THE SUN KISSED SCROLLS

Light Claw

RUBY ELLIS

First published by RUBY ELLIS 2026

Copyright © 2026 by Ruby Ellis

All rights reserved. No part of this publication may be reproduced, stored or transmitted in any form or by any means, electronic, mechanical, photocopying, recording, scanning, or otherwise without written permission from the publisher. It is illegal to copy this book, post it to a website, or distribute it by any other means without permission.

This novel is entirely a work of fiction. The names, characters and incidents portrayed in it are the work of the author's imagination. Any resemblance to actual persons, living or dead, events or localities is entirely coincidental.

Ruby Ellis asserts the moral right to be identified as the author of this work.

Ruby Ellis has no responsibility for the persistence or accuracy of URLs for external or third-party Internet Websites referred to in this publication and does not guarantee that any content on such Websites is, or will remain, accurate or appropriate.

First edition

"The human brain is wired to cope with grief. It knows even as we fall into unfathomably dark places, there will be light again, and if we just keep moving forward in one brave straight line, however slowly, we'll find our way back again."

—The Two Lives of Lydia Bird by Josie Silver

Content Warning

This book contains strong language, sexually explicit scenes, violence, death of a loved one (off page), kidnapping, injury, & light Dom/Sub dynamics.
Light Claw is intended for readers 18+.

Pronunciation Guide

Mo Chridhe: (mo kree-uh) is a Scottish Gaelic phrase translating literally to "my heart" and is widely used as a term of endearment.

Table of Contents

Prologue	1
1: The Night that Changed Everything	3
2: The Prophecy	12
3: The Night that Changed Everything...Again	17
4: Pissed	26
5: Am I a Disney Princess?	31
6: All That Glitters is About to Explode	40
7: Stud	45
8: My Heart	48
9: A Violent Eruption	52
10: The Mate Fate Picked	59
11: Moon Touched Mended	65
12: Midnight Orientation	77
13: That's New	89
14: Prophecies & Problematic Kisses	100
15: Crash	106
16: Honey	117
17: The Prettiest Peen in the Bunch	122
18: A Big Deal	131
19: Count	142
20: Sex Dungeons & Stalemates	150
21: Drop It Like It's… A Lot	160
22: The Lady With a Screaming Pussy	171
23: Did We Just Become Best Friends?	178
24: Dinner and a Show	189
25: Bared & Bound	198
26: Blood Betrayed	210
27: Claws Out	216
28: Kneeling & Healing	226
29: Piercing Tradition	233
30: Heart Wide Open	240

31: Heat & Eat	250
32: Outnumbered	256
33: Steeling Hearts	267
Epilogue	273
Author's Note	281
Bright Paw Sneak Peek	283

Prologue

Callum

(25 Years Ago)

"Sleep well, little one. Tomorrow when you wake, you will be another year older." My Nana's voice soothes me while I snuggle into my warm bed.

"Will I get a special mark like you?" I reach my hand out to trace the Sun Kissed marking that decorates my Nana's face.

"No, love. You will not receive a Sun Kissed mark. But you are just as important to our family line. One day, when you are older, you will protect our family and ensure that the Sun Kissed blessings remain in the next generation of Claw bears."

"I will?"

"Yes. I have seen it." She places a kiss on my forehead before turning to leave my room at our keep.

"Are you sure I won't get a mark?" I try to keep the disappointment out of my voice, but she hears it anyway.

Nana walks back over and kneels beside my bed. "The females in our family wear a golden mark as proof of their power. But you, my dear grandson, have power in here." She places her hand over my heart. "Your heart holds the greatest power of all. Stronger than any other magic."

"Will my heart sing like father's?"

"Yes. And when it does, you must listen to it."

Nana's voice begins to sing a haunting lullaby, spinning a tale of pain, bravery, and love. I let the words sink into my soul as I drift off to sleep.

1
The Night that Changed Everything

Callum

Walking through the large wolf village of Night, it is amazing to me how so many people are able to live in such proximity to each other. Everywhere I look, more shifters appear from doors and alleys to greet my clan. As far as I am aware, this is the first time that a bear clan has been invented into this mecca of wolf culture.

Long before this village was formed, our peoples lived together—bear, wolf, panther. We were all created by The Mother. We thrived by sharing the land and The Mother's many resources. Over time, our peoples split apart. Our predecessors fought and decided to redistribute territories based on species. The wolves split themselves into packs.

The panthers into family groups. And the bears—we split ourselves into clans.

The Mother Blessed The First Bear with a shifted form and split his heart in two before placing it in another. That is how the pull of a Heart Mate first began. Once she was found, The First Bear joined with his Heart Mate and sired three daughters. Each daughter was kissed by The Sun, granting her a special power. Those three daughters were given a Heart Mate, producing heirs and adding to the population. Over time, bear shifters were born and spread throughout the land, organizing into clans but never settling into large communities.

For the last several years, clans have begun to war with their neighbors. Clan versus clan—fighting over control of the land that belongs to us all.

Six years ago, my clan was exterminated. I was away on a mission—my grandmother had sent me to procure a rare herb that she needed for a medicine. While I was gone, my entire family was killed—father, mother, grandmother, and baby sister.

Mine wasn't the only family that this happened to. All clans with direct lineage to The First were targeted. Out of the twenty or so clans who were still guaranteed to pass Sun Kissed magic through their lines, there are now only three of us that survived.

We were forced into the shadows—slowly building our clans out of trustworthy, dependable bears. But with the damage that the war has done to The Mother, it is time for us to return to the light.

As the Clan Chief of Claw, I will help my people end the war. It is from those efforts that I have now found myself in Night—on my way to meet with the Pack Alphas and their families. I am here to strengthen our alliance with the wolves and hopefully move one step closer to peace in our homeland.

"The Alphas have requested that we meet them in the gardens at the back of the lodge," the Nightfury Beta, Boone, tells me.

I first met Boone over a year ago when he was hunting down his brother, Briggs, who had gone rogue and had a bounty out on his head. Briggs had escaped into bear territory and with our combined efforts, we located him in a tunnel system that I had knew from my childhood. Despite Briggs slipping past us, an alliance between the wolves and my clan had been formed.

It is my hope that an alliance with the wolves will help strengthen my clan to the point where others will not be so quick to attack us. We are low in numbers, but fierce in heart.

"Will all three Alphas be present?" I ask Boone.

"Yes. Along with their True Mates and children." I release a breath. Clearly the wolves plan for this to stay peaceful if they are having their Mates and children to be included. It is how it should be—but I have been living in a war zone for many years, and I do not easily trust.

"All three are Mated?" I ask, not having paid much attention to the lives of the wolves for the last several years.

"Yes. And Moon Touched." Interesting. If I remember correctly, Moon Touched wolves are as rare as our Sun Kissed bears. However, instead of magic being passed down through the family line from one female to the next, Moon Touched magic was gifted to a select few True Mates upon creation.

True Mates for wolves are the equivalent to Heart Mates for us. I have long ago given up the idea of finding my Heart Mate. I have traveled all over the land and have never felt the pull. Once the war settles down, I will find a female to further my line. Without a Heart Mate, it is unlikely that my family's Sun Kissed magic will pass on to any females who are born, but it is still my responsibility to try.

"Is there anything else that I should know before meeting the Alphas?"

Boone thinks for a moment before replying. "Nightfury Alpha, Bade, is who will most likely greet you. His pack is responsible for the wolves' military. His Mate, Reese, will stick close to his side. They have three young children. Their oldest is six and has already found her True Mate. He lives separately on the grounds but will most likely be present during the meeting—at a distance."

I do not know if it is common for wolves to find their Mates at such a young age, but it can be for bears. Most are found before late teens. Or, that it is how it used to be before so many were taken from the world by the rebels.

"Nightfang Alpha, War, has black hair," Boone continues. "Nightfang is made up of mostly hunters. He might wish to discuss changes in herd movements during your stay. He has triplets with his Mate, Rowan. Of the three sisters, she is the most outgoing.

"Nighthowl Alpha, Griffin will most likely want to ask about bear culture. His pack is made up of artists and crafters. He loves to study old texts. He has taken a recent interest in bear culture and has been pouring over all of the information his library has on the topic, limited as it may be. Oh, and maintain distance from his Mate, Ramsey, if possible. He is very protective over her, especially now that she is pregnant."

Absorbing everything that Boone shared, I am grateful that I will have some sense of who everyone is before meeting them. In the last year, I have heard many stories about the Alphas and their Mates—but some of those stories are so strange, they must be exaggerations.

Boone and the other wolves in our procession take us around to the back of the lodge, a large permanent structure like my family's keep, and into a beautiful garden vibrant with life. Off to the side, I notice a handful of children playing together.

Four of my most trusted males—Tor, Bo, Adan, and Colt—keep a steady presence behind me as I approach the group of Alphas.

Just as Boone said, Bade steps forward from the group to greet me. He is holding a squirming infant in his left arm as he extends his right hand in greeting.

"Welcome to our home," he tells me.

"It is nice to finally meet you," I respond. Between the unrest in my territory and a whole list of undertakings that the wolves had to deal with in the aftermath of Briggs' attack, this meeting is a year in the making.

Still clasping his arm in mine, a breeze blows by, carrying a scent that does not exist anymore. It's impossible. Looking around, I notice a young female sprinting towards me. Her chocolate hair is a match to my own. Her golden eyes are ones that I could never forget.

"Juniper?" Her name, one that I have not spoken out loud in years, leaves my mouth in a strained whisper. "But how can this be?"

Bade's Mate, Reese, steps forward passing the infant that she was holding into Bade's arms while she intercepts Juniper. "Do you know Juni?" she asks me.

Before my tongue can catch up to my brain, Juni answers. "This is my brother. I have seen him in my dreams, but I didn't know they were *real* dreams."

Dreams. It is then that I notice the Sun Kissed mark on her temple—exactly like our grandmother's mark.

"I thought you...I came back and everything was burned. Everyone was gone. How did you survive?" My eyes scan her tiny body, looking for any indication that she suffered at the hands of the rebels that night. Burn marks. Scars. But she is fine. Wholly and completely okay—at least on the outside. If I would have known she was alive, I would have searched for her. Has she been alone this entire time?

Reese explains how my grandmother received a vision and was able to escape the attack with Juni. She was only an infant at the time. After my grandmother passed, Juni followed her heart string, which led her to her new family and her Heart Mate. I can't believe how strong and brave my little sister was at only four years old.

"Can I...can I hug you?" I ask Juni.

"Of course, silly. You are my brother. This is how we were supposed to meet again," she says with a giggle.

As I open my arms to pull her in for a hug, Reese's hand grips my arm and her eyes begin to glow. Behind me,

Tor, Bo, Adan, and Colt shift their weight and prepare for an attack. Bade steps forward as well, growling at them.

"What is happening?" I ask, confused.

"It's okay, Cal. This is the good part," my sister tells me with excitement in her eyes.

"Stand down," I tell my men, trusting that nobody would launch into an open attack with so many children around.

Reese continues to glow in front of me as she begins to speak—repeating the same words over and over. "Bruins Mountains. Large lake. Next full moon. Dark hair. Pale skin."

What in the Sun Goddess is going on?

It is then explained to me that Reese has found my Heart Mate. Apparently, her Moon Touched magic allows her to help wolves find their True Mates and touching my skin triggered a vision as to where I will find mine. She will be in the Bruins Mountains by the large lake during the next full moon. My Mate has dark hair, pale skin, and, according to Reese, she looked scared. My heart twists at the thought of my Mate being alone and scared. I need to find her.

I know exactly which lake Reese is talking about. The Bruins Mountains are a large chain of peaks that boast several bodies of water. However, there is only one lake that would be considered large. And, unfortunately, it is a favored spot for enemy clans to gather. I need to find her before she is found by someone else.

I have 10 days before the next full moon and about 7 days of travel. We will need to leave tomorrow to arrive before she does.

"Is his Mate a shifter?" I hear a quiet voice ask, looking over my shoulder to see Ramsey stepping forward.

What? Of course she is a shifter. Everyone here is a shifter. Right?

Reese shakes her head and my eyes go wide with this new information. What is happening?

I follow the wolves and their families inside, quite honestly moving on auto pilot as I process the idea of my Mate not being a shifter. I did not even know that it was possible. I look over at Tor, my cousin, who shakes his head and shrugs to let me know that he is just as confused as I am.

We enter a large, comfortable sitting area and take our seats while an elderly female scoops up the infants and ushers the toddlers out of the room. Juni stays with us, climbing onto Bade's lap while we all settle in for the wildest story I have ever heard.

2
The Prophecy

Callum

"So," I say, trying to digest all of the information that was just heaped in front of me. "What you are telling me is that Rowan, Ramsey, and Reese all came from a different world. Your souls pulled them here. You have all been blessed with extraordinary powers. And now, the infertility issues that the wolves have been plagued with have started to reverse."

"Exactly." The Alpha from Nighthowl, Griffin, has been the one to share the most. "I found an excerpt from The Mother foretelling their arrival—but only after they were already here. Here it is—" Griffin opens a journal to show me the prophecy. "It reads:

> And there were Three
> Goddesses of the Moon

> Born among Man
> Awakened by Love
> To Bear, Mend, and Find
> To Restore the Balance
> To Replenish The Mother
> Divided, together once more
> Hearts will Bind

"If your Mate is human, like my Mate and her sisters, it is likely that she was sent with a similar purpose."

"Cal," Tor says. "If I may?"

"Of course," I tell him. Similar to Griffin, Tor has spent most of his time maintaining records and preserving texts about our world.

"There is a poem that I am aware of that might explain the arrival of your Mate from another world. The mention of 'three' as well as the 'goddesses of the moon', that references Moon Touched, correct?"

"Yes, we believe so," Griffin shares.

Tor nods. "This poem has been passed down in my family's line. Our family has always been made up of storytellers—memory keepers. We no longer have Sun Kissed in our line, but because of our knowledge, we have remained close with those who do. My aunt, Callum's mother, was a memory keeper as well. Perhaps the poem is not simply that, but a prophecy as well. The poem goes like this:

> Symptoms of The Mother Cursed

> With Rapacity's Blight
> There will be Three Sons of the First
> Aided by a Sister's Might
> Who will Rise from the Shadows
> Back into the Light
> Together as One
> Claw, Paw, and Maw
> Will Fight the Bane
> Will Start their Reign
> And Rid The Mother of her Pain."

"A Sister's Might? Juni?" Bade asks, a protective growl rumbling from his chest.

"Possibly—though I think that it is speaking more generally of the Sun Kissed. Juni is my sister, but being Sun Kissed, she is also a Sister of The Mother," I explain.

"'And on the eve of their fifth birthday, The Sun will shine down and bestow a kiss upon the blessed, forever marking her a Sister of The Mother.' That is the passage that I found about Sun Kissed when we were looking to learn more about Juni. We were trying to find out all we could about her powers." Bade explains.

"Juni is only six. If the prophecy is referring to her—I'm sorry but she is just too young. She has already been through too much at such a young age," Reese adds. Her protective words about my little sister make my chest warm.

"It's okay, Mommy," Juni says as she crawls into Reese's lap. "I will help Cal if he needs it. But I haven't seen it," she adds firmly.

"In your vision, did Callum's Mate have a Sun Kissed mark?" Ramsey asks her sister.

"Not that I noticed. But she was wearing clothes. It is possible. Do the marks always show up on their temples?"

"No. That is specific to the women in my family line, I believe. The Sun Kissed powers transfer from female to female," I explain. "Juni has visions. Our grandmother had visions. Her mother before her had visions. So, all their markings are the same. But someone from a different line might carry their marks in a different location on their body. Like how your moon markings are different from your sisters because your powers are different."

"Regardless of whether your Mate is Sun Kissed, you will still need to find her. And soon. Humans are fragile in this world. They cannot heal like we can." Griffin's reminder of my Mate's mortality urges me into action.

Looking over at my clan, I make the decision that we will leave at first light. Joined again by their young children, the Night family shares a meal with us and ensures our comfort in their guest rooms.

We do not have the ability to speak mind to mind like the wolves, so I sent a message with my falcon to Claw Keep letting the rest of the clan know that our return will be delayed. I have not yet let them know that Juni has been found alive. I do not know how everyone will feel about me leaving our heir with wolves instead of bringing her back home to keep safe.

It is clear to me that Juni belongs with the Nights. They might not be blood, but they are her family. They will protect her. And bear territory is much more dangerous than the land that the wolves inhabit.

Unrest between clans has been an issue for years—but if that poem is in fact a prophecy, things are about to get worse before they get better.

3
The Night that Changed Everything...Again

Willa

"Another?" I ask one of our regulars, Bill, as he peels the label off his Bud Light. He gives me a nod after I have already reached into the cooler for a second bottle and adds some more cash to the pile sitting in front of him.

I have been working at Lucky's Pub for the last few years. If you had told me five years ago that I would be slinging drinks at a bar in Chicago instead of kicking ass in the courtroom like I had planned, I would have laughed in your face.

Unfortunately, I had not planned on needing to drop out of school and move back into my childhood home to take care of my grandma. When I received the phone call from the hospital, letting me know that she had fallen and called herself an ambulance, I didn't hesitate to return home.

Mabel Fort raised me.

When my mother left me at her door when I was a toddler, she took me in without question. She worked two jobs so that I didn't go without. She helped pay for all four years of my undergrad and helped subsidize my housing so that I could live closer to campus.

It was supposed to be a one semester break while she recovered from her hip replacement. Something that I could easily make up over a summer semester and by adding extra classes in the fall.

But life had other plans. My grandma's hip replacement turned into complication after complication. She never regained mobility. Her health declined rapidly and I couldn't leave her. She told me that I needed to go back. That she was fine with a home nurse providing her care. But I couldn't do it. My grandma needed me now just like I needed her then. So, I stayed. I pushed my extended leave another semester—just to give us more time to get her healthy.

Not long after the start of the fall semester, she passed away in her sleep.

After her funeral, I returned to my childhood home hoping to find an answer as to what my next move should be. I couldn't return to law school until the next semester. My bank account had been almost completely depleted while I focused on my grandma's care.

Mindlessly rifling through a stack of mail, I found the only secret my grandma ever kept from me. And it was a big one. She was in debt. So much debt. Digging further into her important documents, I discovered unpaid bills totaling thousands and thousands of dollars and a loan that she had taken out on the house. Without me realizing, my grandma took out several loans to pay for my schooling. Loans that dated back to when I was still in high school. Loans that I had no way of paying back.

Once the shock wore off, I realized that I really only had one option. Most of the debt was wiped away with her death but if I wanted to keep the house, I needed to get a job.

That seems obvious, right?

Casting a wide net, I sent my resume out to about fifty different employers. I did not have any real work experience, but I did have an undergrad in political science and two years of law school under my belt. Surely someone would want to hire me.

After several rejections, I walked into Lucky's Pub hoping to drown my sorrows with a pint and some onion rings. An hour later, I had soaked the bar top in my tears and was offered a position mixing drinks. The owner had apparently known my grandma and took pity on me. But I can't really complain. Declan "Lucky" Byrne is a kindhearted older gentleman who pays decently and does not get handsy behind the bar. Because of my impromptu mental breakdown on said bar, he is aware of my monetary crisis. He gives me as many hours as possible and has no issue with me taking time off to interview for other jobs.

Bill cuts himself off before I am forced to take his keys and settles his tab with me. Placing the tip into my jar, I try to calculate how much I have earned tonight. It looks like about one hundred bucks—which is okay for a random Tuesday night. But it is not enough to pay the bills and get the groceries that I desperately need.

"Hey Boss?" I speak loud enough so that he can hear me over the music. "Are there any more shifts that I can pick up this week?"

His eyes soften and his mouth tilts into a small frown. I know his answer before he says it. "You already took the extra shifts that I have. I can't give you any more without taking something away from someone else."

My shoulders slump and I nod my understanding.

"Hey babe!" My head whips towards the door as I hear my friends' voices above the general noise in the pub. Leaning over the bar top, they each pull me into a hug before settling down on two empty stools.

"Hey guys! What can I get you?" I offer them a smile even though I am still upset about the state of my bank account.

"Two old fashioneds, but make them young," Freya says as Sloane snorts and pulls out her card to start a tab.

"Have you eaten?" Sloane asks as I begin mixing their Shirley Temples, adding extra cherries to one because Freya prefers it that way.

"Yes, Mom." I tell her with an eye roll. "I had a granola bar before I started my shift."

"That was hours ago! Lucky, are you not letting our girl eat?" Sloane playfully glares at my boss.

"She refuses to take a break." He shrugs, knowing that her displeasure is completely directed at me.

"Willa, you know that you need to eat to maintain your strength. We do not need to put any unnecessary strain on our tickers." Freya moves her hand to my forehead. "Are you feeling okay? You are all sweaty."

I have known Freya and Sloane for most of my life. After discovering my congenital heart defect, my grandma signed us up for a local support group for families in similar situations. My doctor recommended it to us when he realized that we did not have any support other than each other. While it was sometimes awkward to meet up in a church basement while the adults shared their fears and stuff, it was where I met my friends, so I will always be grateful.

I swat at her hand. "I'm fine. I just got a little stressed remembering that it is the middle of the month."

My friends give me sympathetic smiles. They are fully aware of my low funds and are always offering to help me cover some of the payments. But I can't accept their help. While they both come from money, they have their own lives to fund. They do not need to pay back the debt that my grandma went into because of me.

"Lucky, put in a triple order of those Reuben sliders that Willa loves so much. If she refuses to take a break, we will just force feed her while she works." Sloane gives Lucky a wink, which he returns. Traitor.

My pride urges me to refuse the meal, not wanting the pity. But I know that I will be returning home to an empty fridge in a few hours, so I suck it up and devour my dinner. I even sit down and drink some water when Lucky not so subtly leads me to sit in a booth with my friends.

"So, what's new pussycats?" I ask, knowing that my besties will chatter away and distract me from my stress.

"I had another awful date last night," Sloane shares. "My parents set me up with another one of their pre-approved future husbands."

"Blech. I can't believe that they are still doing that," I tell her. As soon as she turned 18, Sloane was paraded around country clubs and bougie parties by her parents in hopes of finding her a suitable husband.

"They won't stop until I find someone," she groans.

"What was this one like?" Freya asks.

"He picked me up from my parents' house because I did not want to give him my actual address—"

"Smart," I interrupt.

"It isn't my first rodeo," she says with a mouth full of slider. "Anyway, he brought flowers for my mother, stared at my rack instead of my face, called me Suzy, and told me that we would ideally have two sons shortly after our spring wedding when he will take my virginity. We hadn't even gotten our appetizers yet."

"What did you say to all of that?" Freya asks.

Sloane pops a cherry in her mouth. "Obviously, I told him that I was already pregnant with my drug addict boyfriend's baby and asked him if he would love it like his own since we were clearly destined for each other, like the mature 24-year-old that I am."

I snort. "Real mature. Almost as good as the time that you faked cardiac arrest because Poindexter Number 3 asked you to marry him on your second date."

"Oh yes, back when I was young and believed everyone deserves a second chance even though they spent their entire first chance sweating profusely and mumbling through small talk."

"I still don't know what your parents were thinking with that one. You would have eaten him alive," Freya adds.

"Ew. My mouth was never going to get close enough to take a bite."

Freya and I both laugh.

"Now," she continues, "they are getting desperate because my internal clock is counting down and if my dates don't just assume that we will be getting married, they aren't good enough for me."

"Well, sure, your eggs are drying up as we speak," I add.

"Also, who wants to tell them that you lost your virginity in the back of a Toyota Corolla at 17?" Freya chuckles as she asks the question.

"Ooh! Me! Pick me! I volunteer as tribute!" I shout as I wave my hand high in the air like a nerd.

"If we tell them the truth, they will try to send me away to one of the religious camps that offer sharing circles with a side of exorcism."

"Okay, fine. We will let them think that you are pure even though you are the biggest hoe-bag out of the three of us."

"And that's why I love you." She tells me as she boops my nose.

I begrudgingly admit to myself that I am feeling better after eating something and taking a small break. Knowing that they will stay to give me a ride home in a couple of hours, I say a quick goodbye to my friends and return to my spot slinging pints behind the bar.

The rest of the night is filled with fulfilling the occasional order and mindlessly wiping down the bar as I contemplate other ways to earn some quick cash. I made a promise to myself that I wouldn't resort to selling feet pics on the internet but desperate times and all that. Shaking those thoughts free, I look up at the clock.

"Have a good night, Boss Man!" I wave over my shoulder. With my feet aching, I trudge over to my friends now that I am free to go for the night. Lucky always stays to lock up since his apartment is above the bar. Piling into the backseat of the hired car that Sloane's parents insist she uses, I rest my head against the cool glass of the window.

Sloane and Freya chat quietly about the new art piece Freya is working on and the upcoming show that her artwork will be featured in. I allow my eyelids to droop closed until the bright lights of headlights shine through the darkness. I have only a few seconds to cover my friends' bodies with my own before the crash turns my world black.

4
Pissed

Callum

We have run hard for the last four days, stopping only when we were starving and dead on our feet. So far, we have not run into any clans who have tried to give us trouble. But the closer that we get to our destination, the more likely we are to come under attack.

Claw Keep is only a day's run from the Nightfury Tempest outpost. But to get to my Heart Mate by the full moon, we need to cut more directly across the land, entering straight into lands that are currently controlled by rebel clans. The path that we routed only veers off slightly to avoid known enemy camps. Now that we are deep within enemy territory, our once direct path has begun to zig zag up into the Bruins Mountains. So far, we have made expedient time, not running into any rebel clans, and should arrive two days ahead of the moon.

"Being ahead of schedule should give us time to clear out any threats before your Heart Mate arrives," Tor says as I ready myself to take the first watch for the night.

"That is the plan, though I can feel something brewing in the breeze." He nods, feeling the shift as well. There is still not anyone in range, but the mountains have always been able to sense a threat before our senses would pick it up. All we need to do is listen.

"All those things the Nights said about humans and other worlds…do you think any of it is true?"

His question disorients me a bit. There was never a moment when I questioned the validity of what they told me. Their Moon Touched markings were clear—so that part is true. The women were all speaking in a language I had never heard before, though I could understand it just like all shifters would be able to. Their scents were combined with their Mates, but they did not smell like they had a wolf or beast within them. And I know that she is only six, but Juni would not have lied to me. She recognized me as her brother even though she had been a baby when I last saw her.

"I think it's all true," I admit.

"What will you do if your Mate is not a bear? You know that the clan will want you to produce an heir to continue the line."

"If this female—woman—is truly my Heart Mate, then she is my Heart Mate. It does not matter to me if she can shift or not. Heart Mates are revered above all else. You know that. And if that poem is really a prophecy, then she may have magic of her own just like the Night females."

"And if she does not carry a mark?"

"Then she is still mine and she will be respected as my Mate. When and if she is interested in cubs, we will make that decision together. Our line is secured with Juni as well."

"Yeah, but she is living in a pack now. It is doubtful that my mother will be happy about that." Tor is right, of course, but it doesn't change anything.

"It is not for her to decide what is best for Juni." My words come out as a growl. I understand that he is trying to provide me with another perspective, but I am the Clan Chief. It is my responsibility to do what is best for the clan, even if not everyone agrees with me.

Tor scoffs at my tone but lets it go, knowing that he needled me just a little too far.

I understand there are certain members of my family who would like to push me into mating with specific she-bears to not only further the line, but to also broker peace. And maybe I was considering it since I have searched for my

Mate for several years without any luck. But now that I know my Heart Mate is out there, there is no world in which my bear would let me even get close to a different female—let alone breed one.

Far in the distance, a twig snaps under an errant foot. My ears track the noise as I quietly shift into my bear, signaling to the others in our group that danger is near. As we all take our places around the camp, I let my scent travel through the air, hoping that our company is intimidated and chooses to continue past us without a fight.

Unfortunately, for them, they do not make the right decision. Minutes after hearing the twig snap, our camp is surrounded by a clan of rebel bears. Taking on two opponents at a time, the five of us quickly neutralize the threat, knocking most of the clan unconscious while keeping their leader awake so that we can force him to shift and properly threaten him.

"You dare attack *my* clan in *my* territory?" he snarls at me.

"We are just passing through. It was you who tried to sneak up on us in the middle of the night like cowards when you could have welcomed us during the day," I reply honestly.

"You do not belong here," he growled. "This land belongs to me."

"The Mother belongs to us all." I keep my voice low and steady but push my dominance into my words. The rebel begins to shake, trying to shift to make himself stronger. "Stop." I roar. He stops mid-shift, leaving him in his male form. "Now, are you going to be cooperative and let us move on in the morning or do we need to make the little naps that your clan are currently taking a more permanent affliction?"

The smell of urine fills the air as the coward pisses himself. How any of these clans were able to revolt against our families in the first place is unbelievable to me. I was only 24 when my family was killed and I had more dominance in my little finger than this ancient fool has in his entire body.

Using the ropes and chains that the clan brought with them to capture us, we tie them all up, holding them hostage in *their own territory* until we leave them to lick their wounds at first light.

We do not run into any more issues on our way to the lake.

Staying out of range so that we are not spotted, we make camp in the tall trees that surround the freezing blue water, sending scouts out at regular intervals to ensure that rebel clans do not enter the area without our knowledge.

The full moon is due in two days. With nothing else to do, we sit and wait.

5
Am I a Disney Princess?

Willa

Slowly returning to consciousness, I smile as I feel the warm sun on my face and my lungs fill with fresh air. Freya and Sloane must have opened my bedroom window when they dropped me off at home last night.

Actually, I don't remember getting home. I was so beat after my long shift that I must have fallen asleep in the car. I am always tired—but this painful, bone aching, deep level of exhaustion is new. Hesitantly, I lift my arms up over my head, trying to stretch my muscles back into working order, when the most intense body pains I have ever felt overwhelm me.

My eyes fly open and all of that fresh air from a moment ago is vacuumed back out of my lungs.

I am not in my bed. I am not even in my house. The entire world around me looks like something out of a story book. Picturesque mountains, a crystal blue lake, trees the size of skyscrapers—I must be dreaming.

Sitting up, I reach my hand out to touch the grass that I am laying on. The ground is springy—soft—and dotted with brightly colored wildflowers. Give me a tiara and a talking animal sidekick because I feel like I'm in my Disney Princess era.

Not wanting to leave this dream, but really needing to pee, I pinch myself and focus my energy on waking up. But, after many minutes of trying, nothing happens. I am still sitting in the middle of a meadow next to a giant lake with a full bladder and no idea where I am.

Not having another option, I force my sore muscles into action and stand up, making my way over to the tree line. The tree that I decide is my temporary privacy screen and bathroom is as big as the giant sequoias in California that I always dreamed of visiting. But the leaves are a shimmering shade of purple.

They are absolutely stunning. I am impressed with my ability to dream something like this up.

Not wanting to wake up in the morning having wet my sheets—but not really having another option—I say a quick prayer to the dream gods and relieve myself in a low-lying bush.

Having taken care of business, I gently knead my sore muscles as I walk over to the water's edge to wash my hands in the lake. Standing back up, I take a deep pull of fresh mountain air into my lungs. I am aware that this is all a dream, but it is the closest thing to a vacation that I am going to be able to take in the near, and probably distant, future, so I am not going to waste a minute of it.

I only wish there was a way for my grandma to be here with me. She never enjoyed the hustle and bustle of city life. It is why she lived in the suburbs. But, if she could have lived anywhere at all, grandma definitely would have chosen somewhere like this. On hot summer nights, we would sit in our small backyard and roast marshmallows over a tiny fire. She would tell me about the camping trips that she took with my grandpa when they were newly married. They would take my mother with them when she was little.

It was something that we always talked about doing together, but life was busy with school and sports and the debate team. Then college and law school—it just never happened. Not for the first time, I wish that I would have taken some time to slow down.

I have always been ambitious. Always wanting to prove that I could do the next big, best thing. But now that she is gone, I realize that I never needed to prove myself to her. She was proud of me for just being me.

It makes me wonder why I felt the need to censor myself; to force myself into a perfectly square box of what I thought I should be instead of just being.

Being loud.

Being adventurous.

Being me.

I turn my face towards the sun. I wish that I had more time with her. I wish I could somehow bring her here to this dreamscape and know for certain that she was somewhere she would be happy.

But none of this is real. Other than the gut-wrenching grief that I feel any time that I think of her. In a few moments, I will wake up and she will still be gone. I will wake up and be forced back into the daily grind of scraping by. Alone.

Wiping the very real feeling tears from my cheeks, I suck in a sharp breath as my heart flutters in an irregular rhythm. Having dealt with heart oddities my entire life, I am shocked with how different this one feels. It is like my heart is being jumped back to life, encouraged into a new pattern that almost pulls my attention away from everything else.

When I first woke up in this dream world, the sun was lighting the sky. But now, the sky is a watercolor painting of purples and oranges. And rising high into the sky is a large, full moon. It hasn't felt like that much time has passed, but time probably moves differently here.

Movement catches my attention and I am jolted from the trancelike state that my heartbeat put me in. Turning my head, I see several huge bears walk out from the tree line. Quickly counting, I note at least twenty of them creeping closer to the lake—closer to me.

Knowing that this is all just a really weird dream, I stay rooted to my spot, allowing the bears to quickly eat up the space between us. Do bears even live in packs in real life? I always thought that they were more solitary creatures but apparently dream me is firmly in the 'bears live in herds' mindset.

When one of the bears gets close enough, I reach out a hand to gently pet it on the snout. Why not, right? This might be the talking animal sidekick to my Disney Princess moment. This bear is massive. Much larger than bears are supposed to be. His eyes are unlike any that I have seen before. They are a deep bronzed brown—almost black.

Right before I can make contact, the bear smacks my hand away and lets out a loud roar. Globs of nasty bear slobber hit my face as fiery pain burns my arm.

The force of the bear's paw has left my hand hanging from my wrist at an unnatural angle. Sounds of screaming add to the loud growls and roars that fill the air. It takes a few moments before I realize that the screaming is coming from me.

"Please wake up. Please wake up." I beg and plead with myself to wake up from this nightmare, but nothing happens. Why would my brain do this to me? Before the bear can break any more of my bones, I turn around and run, tripping and catching myself with my already broken and bleeding wrist. "Wake up. Wake up. Wake up!"

There is no possible way for me to outrun these bears, but I keep my feet moving anyway. Behind me, the loud sounds of footsteps get closer—they are charging at me. The entire mob of bears is barreling towards me, and my stupid, scared brain is unable to wake me up.

Stumbling one more time, I scream as the pain in my arm intensifies with a loud crack, signaling another break. No longer able to bear the pain, I give up on running for my life and hope that when the big scary nightmare bear eats me, I will wake up from this hideous turn of events.

Resigning to my fate, I curl up on my side and wait for the inevitable terror that will come.

But it doesn't happen.

After several long seconds, I crack open my eyes just in time to see another flock of bears tearing through the meadow, putting themselves between me and my tormenters, and attacking them in a fierce battle of claws and teeth.

Now that they are distracted, I should get up and run to safety. Even if this is all just a bad dream, I don't *really* want to be eaten by a bear. It seems like a pretty unfortunate way for dream me to go.

Yet I can't look away. My rescuers are outnumbered but they put up a strong fight, taking out several of the offending bears. But it is not without a price. My saviors begin to succumb to their own wounds, and it is not long before it is one on seven. The one being my last hope at making it out of here alive.

The seven remaining bears from the original swarm attack my champion all at once, piling on top of him and biting into his skin with teeth and claws. He puts up a good fight, kicking them off him repeatedly. It is clear that he is much stronger than any of them individually, but this is not a fair fight, and it isn't long before their combined strength begins to overwhelm him. Looking over his shoulder at me while fighting through relentless attacks, he lets out a sorrowful roar that rattles me to my core, shocking my heart, and giving me purpose.

His violet eyes are flecked with gold—a combination of colors that I have always gravitated towards but have never seen in such intensity. The look that he gives me is as much an apology as it is a goodbye.

Remembering that this is a dream, I rise to my feet and dive right into the fray, wedging myself between my rescuer and the dogpile of bears that are still attacking him.

Not having anticipated my move, the offending bears freeze. It is only for a split second, but it is long enough for *my* bear to move. His eyes blaze with panic right before he roars and flips us so that his body protects mine from the enemy claws.

Lash after wicked lash, his back takes most of the beating as he bravely stands over my body.

Crying at the pain in his eyes, I wrap my unbroken arm around his thick neck and pull his body flush with mine. "Please be okay," I whisper into his fur.

Out of nowhere, the dream world shifts again and is tinged in a golden hue as a wave of supernatural power blasts around us, sending our attackers flying in all directions. Scrambling out from under him before he collapses and crushes me, I try to stand and look at the aftermath of this battle.

I can't stop the shocked gasp that leaves my lungs.

Laying close to us, the four other bears that arrived with my purple-eyed beast are slowly starting to stir, shaking their heads as they come back to consciousness. The twenty bears that arrived first are now blown away from us, at least thirty yards from us on all sides. It is as if a nuclear bomb went off and only the good guys were protected from the explosion.

Sensing movement close to me, I turn to look at my bear—the one who protected my dream life with his own—just in time to see him shutter from a bear to a man and back to a bear again. I rub my eyes, not fully believing what I just witnessed. But it doesn't change the image. All around me, the bears flicker between forms.

It is the last thing I see before the dream ends and the quiet blackness claims me again.

6
All That Glitters is About to Explode

Callum

(Earlier that day)

"Two clans were spotted meeting together about an hour away," Adan reports after he returns from his scouting mission.

"Still no sign of the female?" I ask, already knowing the answer.

"Not yet. The full moon is tonight, though. If what the Nightfury's Mate saw is true, she could appear at any time today."

I nod, already having committed the details of Reese's vision to memory. Looking inside myself, I try to locate the thread that will pull our hearts together. So far, there is nothing there. Either this female is not my Heart Mate, or she is not in our world yet. Given how the human sisters in Night appeared out of thin air, I am hoping that it is the latter.

Needing to distract myself and use up some of this anxious energy that is coursing through my veins, I ask Bo and Adan to spar with me. After about two hours, my heart begins to stutter. The pain is excruciating as it seems to stop before restarting and beating at a new rhythm.

Jumping to my feet, I shift into my bear and take off towards the lake, following the golden string that I feel tying my heart to her—to my Heart Mate.

Running close at my heels, my clan and I barrel through the tree line and into the lakeside meadow where my Heart Mate is hurt, curled up on her side as a large group of rogue bears stalk her.

Positioning ourselves between my Mate and her attackers, we are grossly outnumbered. But it does not matter. I will die on this field before I let my Mate come to any more harm.

My clan clashes with the others—each of us taking on three bears at a time. Just like when we were attacked in the forest, we focus our strikes to knock them out, not taking the time to deliver death blows. Full grown bears are incredibly difficult to kill. That is why the slaughter of our families years ago was beyond belief. It was completely unheard of.

We quickly take out as many bears as we can, but it is not long before my clan becomes overwhelmed, succumbing to injuries, and losing consciousness. I watch as Tor falls. The rise and fall of his chest confirm that he is still alive, but I cannot move closer to check on his injuries. I am now the last defense between my Mate and seven rogue bears.

Realizing that I am the last bear standing, all seven bears strike me at once. We form a massive pile of claws and teeth as they gnash at anything they can reach. I force myself to the bottom of the pile, taking on the weight of the bears, but counting on them biting and clawing at each other to get to me.

Looking behind me, I see my Mate watching the fight. I roar at her, begging her to turn around and run. To leave me here on this battlefield and get herself to safety. These bears might kill me, but once my clan heals enough to wake, they will track her down and keep her safe. Tor will bring her to the humans in Night, and she will be safe with the wolves. She just needs to run.

Locking eyes with her, I try to tell her that I am sorry. That I should have been here earlier to save her from the pain that she has already suffered. Her wrist hangs limply from her arm, bleeding and broken in more than one place.

The Night humans told me that without the bond, they could not heal like shifters. If Tor can get her to Ramsey, her arm could be healed with her Moon Touched magic. She could be okay.

I hold on as long as I can, feeling the edge of consciousness slowly slipping from my grasp, but unable to tear my eyes away from my Mate. If this is how I end, I want her moss and gold eyes to be the last that I see.

But my Mate does not run away into the safety of the forest. She runs straight for me, jumping into the battling bears and gluing herself to my body. In a last feat of strength that I muster up from the deepest part of my soul, I turn us so that my body protects her from the sharp slashing of claws that are now ripping my back open.

Holding her broken arm to her chest, she reaches up with the other and pulls our bodies flush with each other.

"Please be okay," she pleads into my fur.

That is when it happens. Her body begins to glow. A bright golden light shines from her chest and erupts, encompassing the meadow in a golden, glittering cloud. The bears at my back are thrown from my body, soaring through the air as if they weigh nothing. My legs shake as my Mate crawls out from under my body, allowing me to collapse to the ground without crushing her.

I lift my head, assessing the damage that the blast did to my clan. But they are laying exactly as they dropped, unharmed by the eruption from my Mate's chest, a few of them groaning as they shake themselves awake.

My Mate stands next to me, turning her eyes back towards me as I shift between forms in an effort to heal myself quicker. She stares at my changing form, rubbing her eyes and blinking rapidly to clear her vision. Once I am certain that the worst of my injuries are healed enough to move, I settle into my male form, wanting to ease her discomfort at our massive forms and to be able to communicate effectively with her.

Her eyes trail over my bare body, settling once more at my eyes before she collapses to the ground, unconscious from shock or the aftermath of her injuries.

Knowing that we have limited time before our attackers reawaken, I lift my Mate into my arms and carry her out of the meadow. My clan follows close behind in their bear forms, guarding my back as I lead us to safety.

7
Stud

Willa

I wake with a scream. The bones in my arms feel as if they have been shattered and the pain is so forceful that tears flow from my eyes and it is hard to catch my breath. I have never felt such severe pain before in my life.

I force my eyes to open, wondering how I am still feeling such pain now that I have woken up from that intense dream. But it is not the walls of my bedroom that surround me. Instead, I see that I am surrounded by the large purple trees that were in my dream.

How have I not woken up yet?

Feeling a cushioned heat against my back, I turn my body so that I am once again face to face with a bear. *My* bear. His eyes are open and I can clearly see the flecks of gold in his deep purple eyes. Until I saw him in the meadow, I had never seen eyes like these. They instantly pull me in, and I almost drown in their depths.

Remembering the awful pain in my arm, I suck in a sharp breath and hold it tightly to my chest, afraid to move it.

"I...I need a doctor." I tell the bear. Unsure if he can understand me. I don't know what the rules are in this dream world where trees are purple and men turn into bears but maybe I will be able to conjure up a doctor or some pain meds or some whiskey. Honestly, anything that will help numb this excruciating pain.

Proving that I was not hallucinating before I lost consciousness, the bear shifts into a man. But not just any man. This man is huge. His skin is deeply tanned, his hair is a chocolate brown, braided tightly along the sides of his head while the center is left loose to spill down to his back. Woven into the tight braids are small, golden hoops. His chest is broad and muscled, tattooed with black swirls and characters that might be a different language. His entire body is hard and defined, as if he was chiseled from stone.

I can't help but mentally pat myself on the back for imagining such a perfect specimen for my never-ending dream.

"A doctor?" I try again, looking up to him as he stands above me. "I need something for the pain."

He crouches down in front of me. "I have some tea that you can drink for the pain, but it will make you sleep. I wanted you to have the option." His voice is low and deep. The words rumble out of him and wrap around my heart in perfect English.

I look around, noticing the four other bears that are resting in a circle around us, as if they are guarding me and my bear—or man, I guess—even in their slumber.

Doing my best to not look below the belt, I return my gaze to the man beside me. "What is your name?" I ask.

His eyes soften towards me. "Callum Claw. But most call me Cal. You can call me anything you like."

I laugh despite the pain. Apparently, my bear man is a bit of a sweet talker. "Okay, Stud. My name is Willa."

8
My Heart

Callum

Willa. My Heart Mate's name is Willa.

She is the most beautiful creature I have ever laid eyes on. Even in pain, her eyes are bright—so brilliant that they light up my soul. Her hair is as dark as midnight, contrasting severely with her pale skin.

Her scent, while tainted with the grime of battle, is the sweetest honey I have ever smelled. There is something else there too. It is more subtle—citrus. Orange blossoms. Willa smells like honey and orange blossom. I hold back a moan, unable to prevent my inappropriately timed arousal, but not wanting to scare her away.

"So, you said something about tea?" Her words pull me out of my thoughts.

"Yes," I clear my throat. "It should help with the pain, but it will make you sleep. I wanted you to be able to choose if it was something you were comfortable with. I am sure that this situation has been jarring for you."

"It is definitely the strangest dream I have ever had," she mutters under her breath. "At this point, I will try anything," she says louder. "The pain is pretty unbearable." She snorts. "Un-bear-able. Get it?" She begins laughing harder, waking my clan from their resting places.

Tor gives me a look from across the camp. *Is she okay?* His eyes try to convey to me. I shrug my shoulders at him. I don't know what the fuck is going on, though her laugh is almost as beautiful as her eyes.

I busy myself by mixing up her tea.

"I'm sorry," she says, panting as she calms herself back down. "I think this whole situation is just catching up to me. I know that eventually I will wake up from this dream and I will be back to slinging drinks at the pub, but right now, you seem very real."

Dream? Does she think that this is a dream?

"I am real," I tell her softly. "This is all real."

"Yeah, okay." She laughs as she clutches her splinted arm to her chest. "This is definitely real. There is nothing *not* real about a giant, gorgeous, naked—" her roving eyes

49

land on my cock and a blush reddens her cheeks, "pierced..." her voice raises an octave as she takes notice of my golden adornments.

After handing her the warm cup of pain relief tea, I stand to my full height, smiling, and letting her see all of me in the flickering firelight.

Willa's mouth gapes open as she takes in my size. Even in this form, I am larger than most others. I take a step back, not wanting her to feel intimidated.

After several minutes, Willa shakes her head, breaking free from the gravitational pull that draws us together, and looks down at her feet. Sinking to my knees in front of her, I reach out and tip her chin back up, forcing her to meet my gaze.

"Mo Chridhe." *My heart.* The name of affection rolling off my tongue as if it was always meant for her.

I can hear as her heartbeat picks up. The gold flecks in her eyes blaze. Her scent becomes stronger. Not bitter—like it would from fear—but heady with arousal. She is intoxicating. I will never get enough.

"This can't possibly be real," she says breathlessly.

I take a chance, reaching out to grip her uninjured hand, and press it to my chest. "I am real. This...we are real," I repeat.

"But I saw you as a bear." She gestures to my clan who have settled back down for the night in their bear forms.

"We are surrounded by bears. This does not happen in real life."

"It happens in this world," I tell her gently.

"This dream world?"

"No..." I start, but then stop myself after recalling what the Nights told me about the human world. I need to explain this to her better. "You are a human—yes?"

"Of course," she says, looking confused. I can tell that the tea has begun to work as her eyes begin to haze over.

"I am not," I say. "Everything that you have seen is real. This world is different from the one that you know. I will explain in more detail when you wake, Mo Chridhe. You must sleep now. Your body needs time to heal."

I stand to retrieve a blanket, hoping that it will make her more comfortable.

"Cal," her quiet voice calls out to me.

I return to her side, sitting on the ground next to her. Wrapping the blanket around her shoulders, she does not protest as I keep my arm wrapped around her.

"Will you stay with me, Stud?" Her head drops forward, heavy with sleep. I reposition us so that she can use my body for support.

"Always."

9
A Violent Eruption

Willa

Peeling my eyes open takes more work than normal. It feels as if my eyelids are made from iron. Expecting to sit up in my bed, surrounded by the same four walls that greeted me for most of my life, I am surprised to find myself still in the magical dream forest. Only this time, the sun is high in the sky, and the trees are moving all around me.

No.

The trees aren't moving.

I am.

Doing my best to not freak the fuck out and fall off of the back of my dream bear, I grasp tightly at the brown fur that covers his back. Looking down at my legs, I see that he has fashioned a seatbelt of sorts out of rope and leather. Kinky.

Suddenly, my stomach catches up with me and the twisting in my gut tells me that I have about 10 seconds before I blow chunks all over the hunky bear-man's back.

"Hey, Stud?" I say, holding my hand over my mouth. "I think I'm going to be sick!"

Without any indication that he has heard me, I am suddenly falling towards the ground, almost faceplanting before strong arms band around my middle and stop my descent. Unfortunately, the pressure on my gut causes my insides to spill from my mouth in a violent eruption.

Still holding me to his body, Cal lowers us both onto our knees, allowing me to tip forward as I continue emptying my stomach.

"I'm so sorry, Mo Chridhe. Let it all out." Cal's large hand swipes my loose strands of hair out of my face before he removes a thin length of leather from his own hair and uses it to tie mine back.

When the heaving slows and the world stops spinning around me, I push back against his body and slide down to sit on my ass. Looking around, I see that the other bears have also shifted into large men and are awkwardly standing around—clearly trying to offer me some privacy. One of the men slowly steps forward, offering Cal an old-fashioned looking water flask. Lifting it to my lips, he encourages me to drink.

"Thanks," I say before timidly taking a sip. My stomach is still feeling sensitive.

"Are you feeling better?" Cal asks, bringing the water to my lips again.

"I think the worst of it has passed. I'm sorry you had to deal with that," I add, feeling embarrassed about the whole thing.

"You do not need to apologize, Mo Chridhe. Not to me. Never to me."

His voice does something to me that I can't quite explain. It is like a warmth that radiates throughout my body, wrapping itself around my very essence. It feels like safety. It feels like home.

"Cal," the Waterboy says, "we need to keep moving."

"We will stay as long as my Mate needs us to," Cal replies. A low growl laced in his words.

Wait a minute. His Mate? What does that mean? I have a hazy memory of Cal telling me that he is not human—the massive bear that he turns into is a pretty clear indicator that he was telling the truth about that. He also told me that this world is different from the world that I know. But isn't this all just a dream?

I think back to everything that has happened since I first woke up in that clearing by the lake. Despite the magic that is clearly woven into the cloth of everything in this world, it does all *feel* real. The air that I am breathing, the warm sun on my face, the strong body that is pressed against my back, the throbbing pain in my arm, which is strapped to my chest—it all feels very real. Did I seriously wake up in a different world?

"Yes, my love," Cal replies softly. I must have asked that question out loud.

"How is this possible?" I ask, my words shake out of me as I start to shiver despite the warm sun. I begin to gasp. No matter how much air I try to suck in, it doesn't reach my lungs.

"Breathe, Willa. I will explain everything that I know. But I need you to breathe."

Breathe. Just breathe. I can do that. Right? It is something that I haven't had to put much effort into for the last 24 years. I should be able to do it now too. Am I having a panic attack?

Cal raises my hand and places it on his chest as I try to mimic his breathing pattern. He lowers his forehead to my own, whispering words in a language that I do not understand, not breaking contact until I have calmed back down.

"There you go," he says, pulling away only far enough to see that the rest of my body is responding to my steady breaths.

"Cal," that other man says again, sharply. "We are about to have company."

Tipping my face back up, he forces me to meet his eye. "Stay behind me. My clan will protect you just as I will. If I tell you to run, I need you to run deeper into the trees. Don't stay on the trail. Run and find a place to hide. We will find you. Do you understand?"

I jerk my head up and down, unable to form words as fear claws at my skin.

"I will keep you safe," he tells me before kissing my forehead and shifting back into his massive bear form—blocking me from seeing anything other than his fur covered back. Needing to feel the comfort that he brings me, I step even closer, twisting my fingers in his coat, positioning myself so that I am still hidden, but can see the path ahead of us.

Waterboy stays in his human form, stepping around Cal and calling out to the forest. "Show yourselves. We know you are here."

Moments later, four bears ranging in shades of black and brown, emerge from the trees and step out onto the path about 50 yards ahead of us. "We are just passing through," Cal's friend says. "We are not looking for trouble."

I feel it at the same time Cal does. The air shifts—just slightly—but it is enough that it causes us both to tense. A branch snaps to the right just as a creak comes from the left. All around us, bears begin to creep closer. We are surrounded and completely outnumbered.

Even if he wanted me to—there is no way for me to run and hide. Crouching lower, Cal stretches his back leg out, creating a ramp for me to climb. Scurrying up onto his back is awkward with only one working arm but I push through the pain. Once I am up high, I can see how dire this situation is. There is no possible way for us to fight our way out.

"Cal, there are too many of them." I keep my voice quiet, not wanting to draw too much attention to myself.

A low growl rumbles from his chest. It is barely audible, but I can feel it rumble between my thighs as I cling tighter to his body. Cal's friend keeps talking, trying to reason with the bears that clearly have no intentions other than to attack us.

Like the snap of a rubber band, the mood in the air shifts again, mere seconds before the ambush attacks. Cal's friends circle around us, protecting me. I appreciate the thought, but I know that it is futile. There are just too many of them and too few of us.

Unsure what is happening, I feel a burning heat pulsing in my chest. Just like in the clearing, I pull myself close to Cal and desperately wish for us all to be okay. At this point, I am unsure as to whether this is a dream—but if it is, I should be able to override whatever fucked up scenario my brain has, yet again, thought up, and turn the tides back into our favor.

"Please work. Please work. Please work," I repeat, repeatedly as the five bears in our group, Cal included, snarl and swipe at our attackers.

The heat spreads from my chest, radiating out into my arms, legs, and head. Having no choice but to trust that this is what is supposed to happen, I release Cal's fur and spread my unbroken arm out wide. A bright, golden glow pulses from my body in short bursts before blasting out of me. I scream as wave after wave of power erupts from my chest, protecting our small group and sending our attackers flying through the air.

When the golden glow recedes, I collapse onto Cal's back—no longer having the strength to keep myself upright. Cal shifts, catching me before I splat onto the turned-up earth beneath our feet.

"Are you okay?" he asks, running his hand over my face, needing to see for himself that I survived whatever the hell that was.

"Hey, Stud," I say with a soft smile before I let darkness take me.

10
The Mate Fate Picked

Callum

She did it again. That same glow that discharged our attackers by the lake saved us just now. I'm not even sure that Willa knows she is the one who did it. It must be related to her Sun Kissed magic—if the prophecy is to be believed. I have not found a Sun Kissed mark on her, but the power seems to radiate from her chest. Her mark is probably hidden by her clothing.

Whatever that power was—it seems to have cost her a great deal. Right after the power receded, she passed out in my arms. We cannot stay here. The blast had bought us some time, but that rogue clan will regain consciousness and attack again if we do not move out of this area.

"Tor, can you carry us both?" I ask my cousin. Riding on the back of another is not something that is typically done, but I do not trust that she will be able to remain on my back in the state that she is in.

Giving me a nod, Tor extends his leg out, creating a ramp so that I can more easily climb onto his back while holding my Mate in my arms. As soon as we are settled, we take off sprinting through the trees, not stopping until we have reached a safe clearing for the night.

Willa is still asleep when we stop to rest. I keep her in my arms, lending her my body heat since we will not risk a fire.

Hearing the call of my hawk, I turn my face towards the sky. Signaling towards Tor, he intercepts my message, allowing me to stay seated with Willa.

"What does it say?" I ask quietly. It only takes him a moment to read and translate the coded message.

"They wish for us to return immediately," he says. "They were expecting us to return days ago and have set up a gathering with 'trusted families.'"

I release a frustrated breath. A gathering of 'trusted families' only ever means one thing. They wish to parade she-bears in front of me. While their intentions are coming from a good place—they want to help the clan by brokering peace with another—it has never worked in the past, and it certainly will not work now that I have found my Heart Mate.

"They will just need to wait. We need to send a message to the Nights, requesting Ramsey's help. I doubt they will enter our territory, but they might meet us at Tempest Outpost."

Tor nods his understanding as he writes the message and sends my hawk back out into the night.

Looking down at my Mate, I am amazed by her strength. According to the Night females, humans are incredibly fragile in this world—but my Mate is so fucking strong. It has only been a few days since she first appeared in this world, but she has already saved our lives twice. She may have thought that she was dreaming, and she might not understand the magic that clearly runs through her veins, but she was brave enough to try.

Slowly unwrapping her arm from the makeshift sling that I fashioned, I check on her injury. The swelling has decreased slightly, but her pale skin is mottled with dark bruises. If she were a shifter, she would have already been nearly healed—especially if she was able to shift between forms a few times to speed up the healing process. But she is human. A being from another world that, if the Nights are to be believed, has no magic at all.

I am desperate to find her Sun Kissed mark—but I was told that humans are more modest than shifters and she might not feel comfortable with me looking at her body—especially while she is unconscious.

That did not stop her from looking at *my* body, though. I smile at the thought. When we get back to the keep, I will need to check our records to see when the next bonding day will occur. The Summer Solstice only happens once per year—and is a day when many Mates choose to bond, but there are other days throughout the solar cycle that can grant us the power as well.

In the past, I have only noted if one of those days was near so that I could make myself scarce from the keep. While my clan would never be able to force me to bond, they are not against letting available she-bears into my private quarters to wait for me in my bed. After finding those 'gifts' several cycles in a row, I tried just avoiding my room. But then they would hunt me down. So now I just leave the keep altogether. With the fighting clans encroaching on my territory, I have been away for several cycles and have lost track.

"After we hear back from the Nights, would you like me to send a message to my mother letting her know that you have found your Heart Mate?" Tor asks, pulling me from my thoughts.

"No," I tell him. "I plan to tell the clan when we arrive back at the keep. I do not need them working themselves into a frenzy before we are back to deal with it."

Tor nods, though his expression tells me that he wants to say more.

"What is it?" I ask.

"You know my mother is going to have an issue with you finding a Mate who is not a she-bear. She has been trying to set you up for years."

I scoff. "If your mother cannot accept my Mate then your mother will have bigger issues than me not choosing one of her pre-approved matches."

A low growl rumbles from Tor's chest before he can silence it.

"Tor, you know that I would not do anything to hurt her. I understand that she means well. But the meddling needs to end. I have found my Heart Mate. Besides, I never had any interest in being set up."

"I know," he grumbles. "She does not realize how pushy she is."

"Oh, I think she knows," I chuckle. "She just knows that she has more leeway with me than she might have with others—even you. She has not pressed the issue of *you* settling down and adding to the line."

"That is because I do not have Sun Kissed magic to pass down," he states. "Your seed is more important to the clan."

"And when the time comes, if my Heart Mate wishes it, we will have cubs. But not before. And certainly not with anyone else."

I understand that my aunt has felt desperate to further our line, but everyone knows that the best chance of securing Sun Kissed blessings in the next generation is through the mating of those destined. Heart Mates. *My* Heart Mate. Willa. Not the many willing females that were placed in my path by my aunt, despite my disinterest in them.

"Please be okay," Willa mutters in her sleep, pulling my attention back towards her as a low pulse of light blinks in her chest.

"Shhh," I say as I gently brush her cheek with my fingertips, trying to soothe her. "You are okay, Mo Chridhe." Her eyes flutter, as if images quickly flash in front of her in her sleep.

Putting her broken arm back into its sling, I hold her a little tighter to my body. Whether she is Sun Kissed or not, she clearly has magic. Powerful magic. Magic that could help us bring peace back to our world.

11
Moon Touched Mended

Callum

Willa has still not regained consciousness by the time we reach Tempest Outpost. We traveled as quickly as we could but had to adjust our route several times to avoid rebel clans. Despite the encouragement from my clan, I have refused to shift and remain atop Tor's back holding my Mate.

At this point, I am unsure if her extended slumber is due to the breaks in her arm or the magic that was used to save us in the forest. I have never seen power like hers before. Even when Sun Kissed magic was prevalent, I do not think that anyone had the ability to clear a field with such force as my Mate can.

I hold Willa tight to me as I slide down from Tor's back.

We are greeted outside the outpost by the Nightfury Beta, Boone, and the two female soldiers that I met previously, Briar and Bree.

"Welcome," Boone says, lowering his head slightly in respect. The female soldiers do the same.

"Thank you for allowing us entrance into your territory," I say. "My Mate is in need of a healer."

"Of course," he nods, gesturing for me to enter through the gates. "The Nighthowl Alphas are waiting inside."

Tor and Bo shift forms while Adan and Colt remain in fur. They will stay outside with the Nightfury soldiers guarding the outpost. While I am certain that the wolves are not a threat to us here, I will not risk bringing danger to their doorstep—and the rebel clans are too unpredictable now to trust that they will not be idiotic enough to try and attack us here.

Before we enter the large, permanent building at the outpost, Boone stops me. "I know that you have met the Nighthowl Alphas—but I ask that your companions maintain their distance from Ramsey."

I nod for Tor and Bo to hang back. They will still follow us in but will keep to the edges of the room. "May I ask why?" I know that she is pregnant, but she has met us all before.

After pausing for a moment, Boone explains. "Before coming to this world, Ramsey lived through unimaginable horrors at the hands of horrible men. It is still something that she struggles with. Being pregnant, and away from home, brings her worries closer to the surface."

I do my best to not let my mind go wild, thinking of what that could possibly mean for my Mate. They came from the same world. Was Willa traumatized like Ramsey?

Following Boone, I carry Willa into the building, crossing the threshold and continuing to a large sitting room. Sitting on a plush chair, Ramsey holds a steady hand to her swollen stomach while her Mate, Griffin, stands behind her.

There are so many physical similarities between Willa and Ramsey. Both women are much smaller than shifter women. Their dark hair and pale skin—even the green of their eyes are such close shades to each other. Despite Willa's being closed, I know that the greatest difference between them are the golden flecks that sparkle like sunlight in my Mate's eyes.

"Callum," Ramsey says, capturing my attention, "It is nice to see you again. I wish it was under better circumstances, though."

I bow my head in respect. Technically, we are on equal footing—but I will forever be grateful for the help she is about to give us.

"Thank you for meeting us here. I would have brought her into your main village, but she has been unconscious for days. She needs immediate help."

Ramsey jumps to her feet, rushing towards us at my words. "I did not realize she has been unconscious. Has she been like this since you found her?" she asks, stretching her hand out to place it on my Mate's chest.

"No," I explain. "The pain relief tea made her drowsy, but she lost consciousness when she used her power."

Ramsey nods, closing her eyes and allowing her silvery magic to flow into Willa's limp body. After a few moments, she pulls back and moves her hand to Willa's broken arm. She sucks in a breath as if she is surprised by what she finds.

When I met with the Nights, it was explained to me that Ramsey's Moon Touched magic allows her to look inside someone's body and mend anything that is out of order. It is utterly remarkable. What she is seeing now, is clearly distressing to her.

"Is she going to be okay?" I ask, needing some reassurance.

"Your Mate's arm is broken in multiple places," Griffin explains while Ramsey continues to focus on her magic. She must be able to communicate with him mind-to-mind while using her magic. "Ramsey is going to piece her bones back together, but it might take some time. Let's bring them somewhere more comfortable." Griffin picks his Mate up, walking side by side with me as we leave the sitting room and find a bedroom to lay Willa down in. The entire time, Ramsey keeps her magic flowing into Willa, not breaking contact even as Griffin sets her down in a chair positioned by the bed.

About 30 minutes later, Griffin speaks again. "Angel, you need to pull back and take a break," he says out loud to his Mate. "You need to save some of your strength."

"Almost," she pants—her breathing has become labored, and she has sweat running down her temples.

"Now, love. You need to pull back now," he tries again.

Seconds later, the moonlight glow recedes from her eyes, and she takes a deep breath. "I have repaired the bones," she explains. "It shouldn't cause her any more pain."

Griffin moves his hand to Ramsey's belly. Seeing his worry, she reassures him. "Our girls are fine, Sweets. I did not use all of my magic. A fix like this just took more concentration than other types of repairs."

Letting them have a moment, I focus my attention back on Willa as she lays motionless in bed. The only real sign of life coming from her is the steady breath that raises her chest and the feeling of her heartbeat beating in time with my own. That is something that I noticed over the last few days of holding her. Our heartbeats are in sync. That chest pain that I felt in the forest before rushing to her aid—the pain that felt as if my heartbeat was shocked into a new rhythm—that is what happened. My heart was magically rebooted to match my Heart Mate's.

"Will she regain consciousness soon?" I ask Ramsey—not sure if she will know but needing to ask anyway.

"I believe so," she says. "You said that she lost consciousness after using her power?"

I nod my head.

"When my sisters and I use our Moon Touched magic in excess, it can cause us to kind of burn out. Our magical well will take time to fill back up. Sometimes that means the magic is not accessible for some time. Other times, it might mean that she will need to rest and eat—refueling her body so that it is strong enough again to support the magic. What is her power?"

"I am not certain. She has used it twice, but it is unlike anything that I have ever seen before—even among the Sun Kissed. It is a kind of golden blast—a forceful cloud that can push others back." I know that I am explaining this poorly, but I continue. "The first time she used it, I was moments away from death. I had 7 bears on my back, tearing into me with their teeth and claws. I was using my body to shield her from the attack. Out of nowhere, she clung tighter to me and then blasted the enemy bears unconscious and completely out of the meadow. The only bears that remained were myself and my clan."

"A shield," Griffin says quietly.

"What?" I ask.

"A shield. You said that you were using your body to shield her from the attack—but her power acted as an even greater shield, blasting everyone at a great enough distance that they were no longer an immediate threat. Her power is an explosive shield."

"When she used her power a second time, was it under the same stress?" Ramsey asks.

"Yes. We were ambushed and were vastly outnumbered. We would not have survived the attack if she did not release her power."

Ramsey nods her head. "Before my sisters and I bonded with our Mates, our magic was unpredictable. We did not have control over when it was used or how much we were able to use. From the research that we have done to learn more about Juni, we know that Sun Kissed magic is not linked to Mates like Moon Touched magic—but it is still possible that her magic is unpredictable right now. We did not have any magic in our world. So, this is all new to her. She might need time to learn how much of her magic can be used at a time to not risk burn out. I couldn't detect any other injuries that would cause her to lose consciousness for such a long period of time. My best guess is that she will wake up once her body has rested enough to support such a great amount of power."

"Thank you," I tell her. If she were one of my healers, I wouldn't hesitate to drag her into my arms for a hug, but remembering Boone's request about maintaining distance, I bow my head in respect instead.

"You are welcome to stay at Tempest Outpost for as long as you need," Griffin tells me. "I know you must be ready to return home—but I am sure that traveling is not ideal with an unconscious Mate."

"I appreciate that," I reply. "This is the first time that I have set her down since she passed out. It will be good to let her rest in an actual bed for some time."

"You have been holding her for days?" Ramsey asks, unshed tears in her eyes.

"Of course. We were in unsafe territory and she was unconscious. I could not risk being apart."

"I would have done the same, Angel," Griffin tells her as he gently wipes the tears from her eyes.

After a moment, Ramsey nods. "You can stay in this room with her. We will make sure that your men have accommodations as well. And we will bring you some food. The bathroom is just through there," she raises her hand to bring my attention to the door across the room. "Would you like help giving her a bath?"

A bath?

"Do you think that is something she would like?" I ask Ramsey. She might not know Willa, but she is more familiar with her customs than I am.

Ramsey bites at her lip as she thinks. "I think that she would appreciate being clean—but humans are more modest than shifters. I would be happy to clean her for you, if that is something that your bear would allow. Or I can help you. But Griffin would need to remain close to me." Ramsey crosses to the wardrobe, pulling out a basic tunic style shirt that the wolves prefer. "I brought some clothing for her from my own closet, but while she is asleep, she might be more comfortable in this."

Paralyzed by the thought of seeing my Mate naked, I am unsure what to do. Ramsey must see my hesitation because she makes the decision for me. "If you can carry her to the tub for me, I will bathe and dress her. You can wait right outside the door with Griffin so that your bear remains comfortable."

Nodding my head, I motion for Tor and Bo to wait in the hall before I lower myself just enough so that I can cradle Willa back into my arms, walking over to the bathroom, and lowering her into the tub. I attempt to leave the room, but my bear forces my feet to remain stuck to the floor. "I don't think that I can leave the room," I tell her quietly. I know that Griffin can hear too—and that is okay—but I do not like feeling so vulnerable.

"You can stand with Griffin along the edge of the room. Just turn your back so that your Mate has a little more privacy. Griff will do the same."

That option seems to be acceptable to my bear because I am now free to step away from the bathtub. Positioning myself at the edge of the room, I try to distract myself by looking out the window. But it is pointless to try. My entire being has been focused on Willa ever since I first felt the shift in my heart.

"Other than her power, have you learned any more about her?" Ramsey asks. I can hear the trickle of water as she washes the dirt from Willa's skin.

"Not much," I admit. "Between the attacks, the pain management tea, and her passing out, we have not had much time to talk. Her name is Willa. There is a good chance she still believes this is all a dream. She does not think that I am real."

Ramsey snorts. "I can understand that. This world is a lot different from the one that we came from. Did she see you shift?"

"Yes. I needed to shift to help myself heal after the first attack. It did not help convince her that I am real."

"Hopefully after she wakes up, I will be able to talk to her," Ramsey says. "Maybe I can help answer some of her questions—one magically transported human to another."

"I would really appreciate that," I tell her sincerely. I cannot imagine how odd this all is for her. It is strange for me, and I wasn't transplanted into a foreign, magical world.

Hearing the water draining, I almost turn around before remembering that Willa might want privacy.

"Okay," Ramsey says. "She is all clean and I have wrapped her in a towel. But I will need help lifting her back out of the tub and holding her while I dress her."

Griffin keeps his back turned as I slowly rotate and then walk to my Mate. Now that she is clean, the contrast between her light skin and her midnight hair is breathtaking. I am desperate for her to open her eyes so that I can see the beauty that they hold again. Making sure that the towel remains in place, I crouch down and lift Willa back into my arms.

Ramsey makes quick work of dressing her in the tunic. It is large enough to fit like a dress on her small frame. Once the fabric is covering her, Ramsey gently pulls the towel free, and I cradle her closely to my chest. "Thank you," I tell her. "I feel so out of my depth. I really appreciate your help."

"You're welcome," she says, reaching out to squeeze my arm. Before they exit the room, Ramsey turns back towards me. "Just be patient with her. I do not know what her life was like before she came here—but even if it was perfect, this is all a major adjustment."

And with that, they leave me alone with my Mate.

12
Midnight Orientation

Willa

I am warm. Too warm. It feels as if I am burning up. A thin layer of sweat coats my cheek as it rests against a molten stone. I must have a fever or something. At least *that* would explain the vivid dream that I had.

Feeling the comforting normalcy of a mattress supporting my body, I realize that my arm also feels fine. No gut-wrenching pain. Not even a dull ache. I let out a breath of relief, raising my arm to cover my closed eyes. The never-ending dream is over. While there were many things that I enjoyed about my fever dream—the hunky, pierced bear man in particular—I can't help but feel thankful that being the victim of another bear attack is no longer likely to happen.

Still feeling exhausted from my fitful sleep, I snuggle down further into my mattress. I am not sure how long I was asleep for, but Lucky will understand if I do not show because I was sick. I will explain it all to him once I work up the energy to peel myself out of my bed.

That was my plan, at least, until I felt my mattress shift beneath me—by itself. It is moving in a steady rhythm, as if it is breathing. My eyes fly open and I scream as I scramble away from the very large, very naked, very real chest of my dream bear man.

Waking, his purple and gold flecked eyes open wide, assessing the room surrounding us for the danger that he believes I am reacting to.

"Wake up, wake up, wake up!" I chant, unsure how to interpret my mixed emotions at the moment. I thought I felt relieved when I realized that this was all just a fever dream. I mean, I did right? I breathed the literal sigh of relief. But seeing Cal, lying next to me in bed—very much alive and real—sends a flurry of butterflies to my stomach and a warmth wraps around my heart. What is happening to me?

"It is okay, Mo Chridhe," his deep voice soothes my panicking soul.

"But my arm," I say. "And the bed. And the fever. It was just a dream. This isn't real."

"This is real, my love. You were injured but you have been healed. Does your arm feel better?"

"But that isn't possible. It was crushed, shattered, broken beyond repair. And that was okay because it was all a dream and I would wake up and none of it would have really happened but every time that I wake up, I don't *actually* wake up. I am still in this dream."

Pulling my hands away from my face, Cal gently turns my chin so that I have no choice but to look directly at him. "I will explain everything that I know. And there is someone here who can talk to you as well. She was in a similar situation not long ago. But I promise you, Mo Chridhe, this is very real." He takes my hands, pressing one to his heart and one to mine. I gasp as I feel our hearts beating as one.

"What is happening?" I ask, my voice barely louder than a whisper.

"What do you remember?"

Once the panic clears a little, I am able to remember. "I woke up in a meadow near a large lake. There were mountains too and trees as tall as skyscrapers. Very different from my home in Chicago."

"Chicago is the name of the land that you are from? Ramsey told me that your world is called Earth."

I'm not sure who Ramsey is—though I must admit that I am glad there is someone who knows that Earth is a thing.

"Earth is the world that I am from. Chicago is a city. Who is Ramsey? Is she here?"

"Yes. She is resting right now—it is the middle of the night. But we can talk to her in the morning. She is the one who healed you with her magic."

She has magic? She must not be human then.

"What else do you remember?" Cal asks again.

"Um. I was attacked by bears. But then you were there—or bear you was there—and you fought but there were too many of them. I tried to change the dream. I thought really hard about how I needed to keep you safe and then it worked. The dream changed and the bad bears were blasted out of the clearing. I saw you shift from bear to man and then the dream world went black. Every time that I wake up, I don't understand how I am still in this dream. None of this makes sense."

Cal swipes the tears from my cheeks. I didn't realize that I had started crying. "Please don't be sad, my love. I promise you are safe with me."

I settle my body closer to him, leaning my head against his shoulder. I don't know how to explain it—but I really do feel safe with him. From that first moment that I saw him in the clearing, he has felt like mine. *My* bear. *My* protector. *Mine.*

"Did you call us mates, or did I imagine that?" I ask after several minutes of silence.

"You remember that, huh?" he smiles as he answers. "Yes. I did call us Mates. Heart Mates, to be exact."

I bring my hand back up to his chest. His heartbeat gives me comfort even though I do not understand why. "Can you tell me what that is? I don't...that isn't a thing where I am from."

"First, I need to tell you that the world that you are in now—while very real—is not the world that you have always known. You are not the first human to appear here, but there are only three others that I know of. They are sisters and are Mated to the wolf Alphas. Ramsey is one of them."

"Okay. And the wolf Alphas—those are like their leaders, right? Are you an Alpha?" I keep trying to remember *anything* that I can about bears, but my very limited knowledge of Chicago's quarterback and tight ends are not going to help me out here.

Cal chuckles. "It is a little more complicated than that, but yes. The wolf Alphas are their leaders. And I am not an Alpha—bears do not have that title. But I am a Clan Chief. That is the equivalent. Our societies are just organized a little differently."

"And the other humans, the sisters...they are all Mated to the Alphas like how you think we are Mates?"

A low rumble emits from his chest before he can stop it. "I am certain that we are Heart Mates."

"Okay, Stud. Calm down. I am just trying to understand. None of this happens in my world," I remind him.

"I know," he says calmly. "I am sorry for growling. Sometimes my bear forces his way closer to the surface. He did not like that you would question our connection to you."

"And this connection…that is why our hearts beat at the same rhythm?"

"Yes, Mo Chridhe. Exactly."

My heart flutters every time he uses that nickname for me. I do not know what it means, but it makes me happy, nonetheless.

"But what does it mean?" I ask.

Cal sighs, not out of frustration or annoyance, but more out of need to explain something that is probably complex as simply as possible so that I do not go running for the hills. "Do you have stories of Creation in your world?"

I nod my head. "Yes. Of course. Though humans can't seem to agree on one. I never really put too much weight into it."

"Well here, in this world, we believe that we were created by The Mother."

"Ooh, a female Almighty—I can get behind that."

He chuckles. "Yes. Why would we believe a male to have created us when it is a female who can bring life into the world?"

"You bring up a real good point there, Stud."

"Like your humans, the story of Creation can vary a bit from species to species—but there are some things that we all agree on. The Mother being the most important. We believe that The Mother blessed The First Bear with a shifted form and then split his heart in two, placing the second half in another. Those two hearts were born separately but pulled themselves together from far across the land. That is how the pull of a Heart Mate first began."

"A Heart Mate? Like a soulmate?"

"Yes. Like the soulmates of your world, we believe in Heart Mates. The wolves believe in soul sharing as well—but they call their Fated Mates 'True Mates.'"

"And our hearts pulled me here? To this world?" I ask, already knowing, deep down, that I am correct. My heart has been pulling me to Cal. I felt it the very first time I saw him. Maybe even before I saw him—when my heart restarted itself and began beating in a new rhythm.

"I believe so. It happened with the Alphas and their human Mates."

"I get a feeling you are going to tell me that there is more," I admit. He is being open with me—explaining everything like he said that he would. But he is also being careful. It is as if he is keeping something from me, not wanting to freak me out any more than I already am.

"There is more. I will explain it all. But I want you to promise to tell me if it becomes too much. This entire situation is a lot for you to learn about in one sitting," he tells me.

"I do better if I know all the facts. It helps me process if I don't feel like things are being kept from me," I explain.

"I can relate to that," he tells me with another smile.

I take a moment to look at him. To truly, take him all in. Other than the glimpse that I got in the forest, when he spun his perfectly naked body around in front of me, I haven't allowed myself to pay too close attention to his body. Mostly because we were not alone. Also, I did not believe that he was real.

His hair is longer than I remember—though it is no longer braided on the sides of his head. A scruffy but hella-hot beard covers his face as if he has not had a chance to shave in a few days. His eyes are the same deep violet that I recall. And his voice is just as soothing as I remember. His chest is bare, displaying dark tattoos on his tanned skin. And he is adorned in golden jewelry. He must not take it off, seeing as he was asleep prior to me screaming and scrambling away from his body. I can't see them now, but I am reminded of other jewelry that I saw on his body when we were in the forest. More specifically, one part of his body. One huge, pierced, part.

Cal sucks in a deep breath, inhaling the air as if it is more vital to him than it was a minute ago. A low, satisfied growl rumbles from his chest and his pupils dilate. There is no way that he knows what I am thinking about…right?

"Are you okay over there, Stud?" I ask, my voice is raspy as I try to keep my cheeks from flushing.

Clearing his throat, he changes the subject. "Are you hungry?"

My stomach takes that exact moment to announce itself to the room. I'm not sure I can even remember when I last ate.

"Yes. Where are we, anyway?" I ask, as he stands, opens the door a crack, and whispers something to someone out in the hall.

Looking around the room, I notice for the first time that we are in a large bedroom. There is an unlit fireplace across the room, along with a door that must lead to a bathroom. The walls are made of logs and stone, kind of like a lodge. The room is decorated, though it is plain, neutral. Most likely a guest room.

"We are in Tempest Outpost in Nightfury territory. Wolves," he says as he busies himself over by the fireplace.

I climb out of bed to join him, sinking down into one of the plush chairs. "Is it okay that we are here?" I don't sense any kind of threat, and I doubt that he would be so relaxed if we were in danger. But it is strange to be in a different species' territory. Right?

"Yes, we were invited here. After you lost consciousness in the forest, I sent a message to the Nighthowl Alphas, requesting their aid in healing you. I would have brought you all the way into their main village if they required me to, but they agreed to meet us here instead. This outpost is the closest outpost to my family's territory."

"And Ramsey, the human that is Mated to the Alpha—she is the one who magically healed me? How is that possible?"

Hearing a soft knock on the door, Cal walks over and intercepts a tray of something that smells like stew. My mouth waters. I did not realize how hungry I was until he mentioned it. Now, I can't stop myself from feeling deep hunger pains. I do my best to not inhale the food and make myself sick.

After I have started eating, Cal sits next to me and continues our conversation. "Yes. Ramsey is a human from your world. I do not know if she is from your Chicago village or from a different one, but she is from Earth."

"But humans don't have magic," I say—mostly to myself, but he replies anyway.

"Ramsey and her sisters are Moon Touched. That means that they received special magic from The Moon. I don't know all the details, but I do know that they did not have any magic before coming to this world. It only appeared after it was triggered here."

I feel as if my brain is going to explode with the amount of information I have learned since waking up, so I focus my attention on my food. I dunk a chunk of the crusty bread into the stew broth and moan as the flavors hit my tongue.

"I'm not sure I have ever eaten anything so delicious."

"I will request the recipe."

Finishing up my dinner, I quickly wash myself up for bed and crawl back under the covers. Cal stands by the fireplace, clearly unsure as to what to do next. Feeling brave, and ridiculously comfortable with him, I pat the open space on the mattress next to me. "Come on, Stud. Don't get shy on me now."

He makes a noise that is somewhere between a sigh of relief and a chuckle before making his way over to me. Climbing onto the mattress, what seemed like plenty of space for him when I offered is dwarfed by his massive body. I have never seen so many muscles on a real person before. It is one of the reasons why I thought that he must be part of a very elaborate dream.

Turning onto my side, I tuck one of my hands under my pillow before laying my other in the gap of space between us. Cal turns to face me as well, noticing my hand, and intertwining it with his own.

"Go to sleep, Mo Chridhe. I will be here when you wake," he says softly.

"You know, I'm really starting to believe that," I say before closing my eyes and allowing the darkness to take me again.

13
That's New

Willa

I wake the next morning to the feeling of Cal shifting off the bed.

For a brief, blissful second, I don't remember where I am. I don't think about who I am or who I was. My body is heavy with the kind of sleep that presses you down into the mattress and makes the world feel far away. Then, reality trickles back in, slow and unwelcome. The strange room. The otherworldly air. The man beside me who feels too solid, too real, to be a dream.

I must have migrated closer to him in my sleep because despite his slow, gentle movement, he can't help but jostle me.

"Sorry," I mumble, my voice scratchy and unfamiliar to my own ears.

"Keep sleeping, love. There is just someone at the door."

The word *love* shouldn't feel like anything. It's just a word. But just like when he calls me Mo Chridhe, it settles into my heart anyway. Warm and grounding. I lift my hand to my chest, trying to hold that feeling inside for just a little longer.

That's when I become painfully aware of the fact that I'm basically naked. The shirt that I am dressed in has ridden up in my sleep, leaving my entire body from the neck down completely exposed underneath the thin blanket that Cal must have draped over me.

I yank the blanket up to my shoulders, clutching it like armor as Cal moves toward the door. My heart starts to race—not from fear, exactly, but from vulnerability. Everything about this world already makes me feel exposed. I don't need literal strangers witnessing a nip slip.

After a brief, muffled conversation in the hallway, Cal glances back at me. "Willa," he says gently. "Are you feeling up for company? Ramsey is here to check on you."

"Oh. Um…" My brain stutters. I can only imagine what I look like—sleep-rumpled and confused.

Seeing my hesitation, Cal turns back to the door and accepts a folded stack of clothing before closing it behind him.

"We can get cleaned up for the day and then meet Ramsey and Griffin for breakfast," he offers. "If that would make you more comfortable?"

I nod quickly, relief loosening the tight knot in my chest. I need time. Time to wake up. Time to think. Time to convince myself that this isn't all going to disappear if I blink too hard.

A dull ache pulses behind my eyes and I wince. My head feels like it's stuffed with cotton and static, like it is still trying to load information it wasn't built to handle.

"Ramsey brought you some clothing as well," Cal says, setting the folded fabric beside me. "We can wash what you were wearing before, if you'd like, but these should fit better than the shirt you have on now. Unless you're comfortable—"

I take his hand before he can finish, the contact instinctive.

"These are great. Thank you," I say softly. "It's just…taking my brain a little longer to catch back up this morning."

He exhales like he's been holding his breath and nods. "Did you sleep okay last night?"

"I did," I admit. "Thank you for staying with me. I don't know why, but I feel safer when you're next to me."

The words slip out before I can overthink them, but they're true. And judging by the small, stunned smile tugging at his mouth, they mean something to him too.

He is nervous.

That helps somehow.

If even the big, confident man who sometimes turns into a bear is unsettled, then maybe I'm not failing at this as badly as it feels.

"Would you like a bath this morning?" he asks, tucking some of my messy hair behind my ear. "Ramsey cleaned you up after she healed you yesterday, but we have time if you want one."

"I don't want to keep them waiting," I say. "Just give me a few minutes."

Grabbing the clothes, I slip into the attached bathroom. The fabric is soft and unfamiliar against my skin, and the mirror reflects someone who looks like me—but not entirely. Like I've stepped half a degree sideways out of my own life.

I probably did.

Dressed in a bralette-style top and a flowy skirt with high slits, I start rummaging through the cabinets. Everything smells faintly herbal and sun warmed.

"Hey, Cal?" I call. "Is this okay for me to use?"

He appears in the doorway as I hold up a tube with foreign lettering. It smells kind of minty, but sweeter.

"Yes," he says, stepping closer. "That's for cleaning your teeth." He finds a small brush and hands it to me.

I thank him and brush while he braids his hair, his movements practiced and unhurried. When he weaves golden hoops into the finished braids, something in my chest tightens.

Admittedly, I haven't seen many people here—not like this, at least—but I'm already certain of one thing.

Cal is devastatingly beautiful.

Not in a polished, untouchable way. In a real way. Sun-darkened skin. Strong hands. A face that looks like it's smiled and worried and worked hard. And his eyes—violet and flecked with gold—feel like they are looking *into* me, not just at me.

He catches me staring but doesn't comment. I clear my throat.

"Are you ready for breakfast?"

He chuckles. "Oh, I could definitely eat."

I flee the room before my brain can finish the dangerous thought about how amazing his stubble would feel against my thighs.

The dining room feels cozy and intimate, which would be great if it didn't feel like I was about to sit for the most important pop quiz of my life.

Cal's presence at my side calms me enough to approach the lady who magically healed me. The woman, who I assume is Ramsey, looks like she could be my cousin. Dark hair, pale skin, green eyes. Her hand rests comfortably on her rounded stomach as she laughs at something the man at her side has said.

That man, who I assume is her Mate, is almost as large as Cal, though he does not seem nearly as intimidating. I am sure that, like everyone in this world, he is able to shift into a fierce beast, but his eyes are kind and he offers me a gentle smile.

I try to relax, but my hands keep opening and closing at my side. I can feel a nervous energy building in my chest, but I swallow it down.

Cal must notice because he reaches down and holds my hand closest to him, bringing his other hand to gently rest on my lower back as he steers me towards the table.

"Good morning!" Ramsey says. "I'm so happy to see you up and moving around. How are you feeling?"

Cal practically places me into a seat before filling a plate and setting it in front of me. I give him a smile as thanks before remembering that Ramsey asked me a question.

"I am feeling okay," I tell her. "Bit of a headache. Mostly confused."

Both Ramsey and her Mate nod like *yes, that tracks.* If what Cal told me about her is true, they experienced something like this not long ago.

"I can check your head after breakfast. My guess is that it is just a side effect of using so much of your magic."

"My magic?" I repeat.

She offers a smile with a nod.

"No. I don't have magic. I have a mountain of debt, a decently strong right arm from waitressing, and half of a law degree," I ramble. "I guess that none of that really matters anymore but what I mean is that I am human."

I look to Cal, wanting him to back me up but he gives Ramsey a barely visible nod.

"Where did you live before coming here?" she asks me.

"Chicago."

"Oh! The Windy City. I always wanted to go there. My sisters lived in NYC. Queens. We were crammed into a tiny apartment, but it was home. Or it felt like it was before we came here."

"And you live here now?"

"Technically, this is my brother's territory. I'm Griffin," her Mate tells me, extending his hand across the table.

"Willa," I respond while shaking his offered hand.

"Oh, gosh. And I am Ramsey. I probably should have started with that. I forgot that you were unconscious when we met before." She lets out an awkward giggle which relaxes me a little. At least I am not the only one who feels weird right now. "I'm sure you have a lot of questions," she continues, "And I am happy to answer any that I can."

Seeing that I have stopped eating, Cal loads up a fork for me and brings it to my mouth. I am so thrown off, that I open my mouth and let him feed me before realizing that I am a strong, independent woman and I can feed myself. Taking the fork from him before he can continue feeding me, I chew another bite before asking my first question. "What did you mean when you said that my headache was probably caused by my magic?"

Cal turns in his chair so that he is facing me. "Do you remember the blast that threw the bears in the attack by the lake. And again, when we were surrounded in the forest?"

"Yes. But…that couldn't have been me. I don't have magic."

"I didn't have any magic before coming to this world either," Ramsey says softly.

"And now you can heal? With magic?"

"Yes. The Moon blessed me with magic. It is rare—but my sisters and I are all Moon Touched along with our Mates." She raises her hands, drawing my attention to the shimmering silver moon phase tattoos that decorate her skin.

I lift up my own hands. "But I don't have a mark. See?"

"Griffin and I had this brought in before breakfast," she says as she stands and walks towards a table holding a large piece of mirrored glass. "This is one of those moments when it would be so much easier if we could take a picture. A little help over here, Sweets?"

Griffin moves over to the mirror and carries it to the table.

"You do have a magical mark. I noticed it when I was cleaning you yesterday. It is not a Moon Touched mark—that is only for wolves. But you do have a Sun Kissed mark. It is right in between your shoulder blades," she continues.

Standing, I maneuver my body so that I can look behind me and see my back reflected in the mirror. Cal stands too, moving my hair so that it drapes over my shoulder.

I gasp. "That's new," I say. Positioned in the center of my upper back, between my shoulder blades, is a large shimmering golden sun. The straps of my top are covering some of it up, so I try to move them. But my hands are shaking so bad that I can't seem to make my fingers grip the fabric. I look over to Cal for help. With gentleness that shouldn't be possible from such large hands, Cal moves my straps from my shoulders down to my upper arms, pulling the band of the top down so that my entire upper back, and the tattoo, are completely exposed.

Blocking my chest from view with his body, Cal presses closer, allowing me to lean against him as my legs begin to shake in shock.

"How is this possible? And why?"

I don't just mean the mark. I mean *all of it*. This world. This power. The way everything seems to have been waiting for me long before I ever knew it existed.

After several minutes of me just staring at my back, Cal helps me re-dress before lowering me back down into my chair.

"Just like how the wolves have the Moon Touched, bears have the Sun Kissed." Cal's voice is steady, calm. "We believe that The Sun, who is a sister to The Mother, kissed a select few with extraordinary magic. The magic is passed down from generation to generation through the women who descended from those first lines."

"But I'm not a bear," I say. I know that it is obvious, but I feel like they keep forgetting that vital fact.

"And I'm not a wolf," Ramsey says. "My sisters and I—you—we were all brought here for a reason. For us, the wolves had been slowly dying out. They needed help. The Moon brought us here so that we could use our Moon Touched magic to Bear, Mend, and Find. My sister Rowan has fertility magic. I can heal. And our younger sister Reese can help wolves find their True Mates through visions."

"Reese is who told me where to find you," Cal tells me.

Something clicks into place. Not comfortably, but undeniably.

I wasn't taken from my old life.

I was called to this life.

The panic still comes when I realize what I did by the lake and in the forest. What I could do again if I give into this building heat in my chest.

"And I have magic that can blast bears like a nuclear bomb?" I ask, my voice hardly audible over the sound of blood rushing through my ears. My breathing begins to feel labored—it doesn't matter how much air I suck in because none of it is making it to my lungs.

"Breathe, Mo Chridhe." Cal presses my hand to his chest and I anchor myself to the steady thrum beneath my palm. One heartbeat. Then another. The same as the beating in my chest.

When the world stops spinning, I look up at him.

"Are you ready for more?" Cal asks.

14
Prophecies & Problematic Kisses

Callum

There is so much more to tell her.

The knowledge sits heavy in my chest, pressing against my ribs like it wants out, like it might crack me open if I hold it in too long. I can see it on her face—the way her eyes keep darting, the way she's bracing herself as if another blow is coming. She is standing on the edge of something vast and terrifying, and I am the one holding the rest of the map.

Do I tell her everything now?

Rip the bandage clean off and let her bleed truth?

Or do I soften it? Shape the edges so they don't cut as deeply?

My bear stirs, a low rumble in my chest. *We do not lie to our Mate.*

I don't miss the reminder. I never would. The bond doesn't allow for deception. And Willa does better when she knows the facts.

Even if knowing can cause pain.

So I steady myself and make the choice I've been making since the moment I found her.

I choose her.

"I can answer your question of 'why'," I tell her carefully. My voice stays calm even as my instincts scream at me to pull her closer, to shield her from what comes next. "Or rather, I can tell you what we know. The reason we think this is happening. But only if you want me to. You are doing so well with all of this, love. I don't want to overwhelm you."

Her mouth twitches, and despite everything, I feel a spark of warmth.

"I think I'm past the point of overwhelm," she says. "Is there a word for over-overwhelm? Because that's what I am."

"Engulfed. Overcome. Swamped," Griffin offers.

I laugh before I can stop myself. The sound surprises even me—rougher than I expect, but real.

"I think I'm all of those," she says, then looks back at me. "But I do want to know everything. Just give it to me straight."

Brave girl. I can't help but think. Not fearless. Brave.

"Just like with the wolves and their reproduction difficulties," I begin, "we are plagued as well. But our affliction is greed. It has poisoned our land." I pause. This next part matters most. "There is a prophecy. If you are all comfortable with it, I can have Tor come in. He knows it better than I do."

They all nod, and I move toward the door. As I call Tor in, I feel the familiar weights settle on my shoulders. The burden of being Chief of Clan Claw. The responsibility of being first-blooded. The pressure of supplying not only survival, but hope.

"Hey, Waterboy," Willa blurts as Tor enters.

I snort before I can stop myself. Goddess help me, she is adorable.

The look of confusion on Tor's face makes Ramsey and Griffin join me in laughter.

"I'm sorry!" Willa apologizes, her face turning red with embarrassment. "I never learned your name in my bouts of consciousness, but you very kindly offered me water while I was blowing chunks and—oh my god, stop talking, Willa!"

Tor smiles, unfazed. "Tor."

"What?" she asks from behind her hands.

He chuckles. "My name is Tor. Well, Torin. But everyone calls me Tor. You can call me anything you want."

The growl escapes my chest before I can cage it.

Willa laughs. "Calm down, Stud. That line only works with you."

My bear preens.

Redirecting her attention back to Tor, she says, "It is nice to meet you. And I will try to remember to call you Tor—but you are pretty ingrained in here as Waterboy." She points to her head as the entire room erupts in laughter at Tor's expense. Serves him right trying to flirt with *my* Mate.

When Tor begins the prophecy, the room quiets.

Griffin pulls out a journal and records the words in Willa's language as Tor says the words out loud.

As the words fill the space, I watch Willa. Watch understanding dawn. Watch the moment when this stops being an abstract mystery and becomes personal.

"Well, The Mother is the land, right? That is what you said last night?"

Clever girl. "Yes," I tell her.

"Rapacity is greed. Aggressive greed," Ramsey adds.

"Yes. I think that it is talking about the greed of the rebel bear clans who are attempting to claim The Mother as their own," I add.

"The bears from the lake and the forest?" Willa asks. When I nod, she turns back to the journal in front of her. "Three Sons of the First... The First bears?"

"Yes," Tor chimes in. "That is most likely referring to the first clans. They are listed later in the poem—Claw, Paw, and Maw."

When she realizes.

"Claw…" she says slowly. "Callum Claw. You're from one of those families?"

"Yes," I say. "Clan Claw is my family's clan. We are descended from The First. And we carry Sun Kissed magic within our line."

The memories press in—fire, blood, the silence of returning home to a lifeless keep.

"There were once many more of us," I continue. "But rebel clans attacked the families of The First. Wiped out entire lines. There are only three of us left. Clan Claw, Paw, and Maw. We went into hiding. Built ourselves back up. And waited."

I don't say *for you.* Not yet.

"And I'm a Sister? A sister of The Sun? That is what the mark on my back means? The Literal. Fucking. Sun. Laid a wet one on me and now I am supposed to use magic that I do not know how to control, to help you fight a war that I don't know anything about and save the land that I thought was just a very elaborate dream up until last night?!"

"We think so," I tell her softly.

"Is there anything else? I'm your Heart Mate, right? Are you going to tell me that I need to pop out babies while I am wielding my make-out magic and saving the world? Because I have to be honest, I can barely keep myself alive. Can you even use condoms with a pierced dick? If I am going to have the complete mental breakdown that I feel coming on, I would like to just freak out about everything all in one go."

"Yes," I tell her firmly. "You are my Heart Mate. But I would never require anything of you. Not this prophecy. Not this war. Not even me. If you do not want any part of this, that is your choice. We will find another way."

"Well of course I'm going to help!" she yells. "But I am going to need a minute to have a meltdown first!"

I can't help but chuckle as my Mate storms out the door and walks out into the outpost. She is going to need that fire for the upcoming war. But first, there are traditions to uphold. A clan to inform. And my aunt to face.

15
Crash

Willa

Heart Mate.

Sun Kissed magic.

War.

I roll the words around in my head like loose change in my pocket, unfamiliar and heavy. None of this was on my five-year plan. This life is infinitely more complicated than slinging drinks at Lucky's and drowning in debt back in Chicago.

But still…I don't feel alone anymore.

That realization lands softly and painfully all at once.

Before this—before bears and magic and destiny with a capital *D*—it was just me. Day after day. Other than my friends, who I miss so much my chest physically aches, I lived alone in every sense of the word. Do you know how depressing it is to finally scrape together enough money to buy groceries, haul them home like a victory prize, and then stand in a quiet kitchen making dinner for one?

Every single day.

No music loud enough to drown out the silence. No one to complain to when the pan burns the food. No shared jokes. Just me, eating leftovers over the sink and telling myself I was fine with it.

That's one of the reasons I didn't mind working at Lucky's. At least there, I was surrounded by people. Noise. Laughter. The low hum of humanity makes me feel like I was part of something, even if I went home alone afterward.

There are plenty of things I am not a fan of in this world—being attacked by homicidal bears is currently the reigning champion—but despite all logic, I feel something here. A strange sense of belonging that I've never felt before. Even growing up, I never felt settled. I was always reaching—toward the next goal, the next responsibility, the next version of myself that might finally feel like enough.

I never stopped long enough to just *be.*

So, I do that now.

In a new world.

In a strange outpost.

On an aggressively uncomfortable bench.

I sit in the present and realize something that sends a small jolt of panic straight through my ribs. *I have never felt more at home than I do when I am with Cal.*

That realization scares me more than the bears and wolves that are guarding this property.

How is it possible to feel this connected to someone in such a short amount of time? How does a stranger become an anchor? My brain wants spreadsheets and timelines and data, but my heart—the disloyal little hussy that it is—doesn't care.

Out of the corner of my eye, I spot Ramsey walking toward me. When she sits beside me, she doesn't try to fill the silence. She just…sits. With me. Like she understands that sometimes being present is enough.

"Did you draw the short straw?" I finally ask. "I'm sorry about my outburst earlier. I'm sure you didn't plan on having a front-row seat to crazy while you ate your waffles."

She laughs, warm and unbothered. "Don't worry about it, Willa. You remind me of my sisters. Rowan, in particular. She would have cackled at you calling a gift from The Sun Goddess 'make-out magic.' She's the one with fertility magic and she goes around telling everyone she has a magic pussy."

I snort before I can stop myself. "She sounds like my friend Freya. Zero filter. No shame."

The laughter fades, replaced by a quiet ache as my thoughts drift back home. To faces I will never see again.

"Do you remember anything from right before you came here?" Ramsey asks gently.

I dig through my memories, sifting through the haze. "I was working. Bartending. I stayed until closing. My friends used to come hang out so I wouldn't have to take a rideshare by myself that late at night."

"They were with you that night?"

I nod. "Yeah. They yelled at me for not eating and basically force-fed me Reuben sliders on my break. Then they stayed until closing. We took a car home—Sloane's family has a car service."

"And then?"

I shake my head. "That's it. Just...lights. Bright lights." My temples throb as I push harder. "Headlights. We were in an accident. I remember throwing myself forward, trying to shield them." My voice breaks. "And then I woke up by a lake and got attacked by bears."

The absurdity almost makes me laugh—but instead, grief crashes in full force.

I cover my face as sobs tear out of me, raw and unstoppable. There's no way my friends walked away from that. It was too fast. Too violent. Too—

Strong arms lift me, firm and unyielding. I'm pressed into a warm chest, breathing in Cal's scent as I focus on the steady rhythm of our hearts. I cling to him like a lifeline, curling impossibly closer.

I cry for my grandmother. For every sacrifice she made so that I could have a chance. I cry for my friends. For whatever fate waited for them after that crash. And I cry for myself. For the baby left on a doorstep. For the teenager who never felt like she was enough. For the woman I thought I would become and now never will.

Cal holds me through it all. He murmurs soft words in a language I don't understand, but I don't need to. I feel the meaning in the way his hands never falter, in the way he *stays.*

When the sobs finally quiet, the sun is high and warm against my skin. I lift my head and press a gentle kiss to his lips.

"Thank you," I whisper.

"Always," he says, kissing away my tears.

"I really will help you," I add weakly. "Sorry about your shirt."

"You can soak me anytime," he replies, adding a smirk. "In fact, I encourage it."

I laugh—ugly, snotty, real.

"Do you want to talk about it?" he asks.

I shake my head. "Not right now. I didn't realize how much I was holding in."

He accepts that without question.

The rest of the day passes quietly. Talking, eating, learning about each other. I officially meet the other members of his clan who are traveling with us. They are all kind to me. Accepting. Not once do they make me feel like an outsider.

Minute by minute, the world feels less sharp.

By the time night comes, exhaustion settles into my bones. Walking back into the cozy dining room where we had breakfast, we are greeted by Ramsey and Griffin.

"I'm so sorry about earlier," I say. I can't help but feel embarrassed.

"You actually handled this all better than most would, I think," Ramsey tells me with a small smile.

"There is no right or wrong reaction to finding out that you were magically transported to a new world," Griffin adds quietly.

Just like at breakfast and lunch, Cal makes me a plate and waits until I have started eating before helping himself. When I notice that Griffin does the same for Ramsey, I realize that it must be some sort of societal custom. Or maybe it is a Mate thing. I am exhausted from the day, so I make a mental note to ask Cal more about that tomorrow.

"If you are feeling up to it, I would like to check you over one last time before we head back to our family's lodge. We plan to leave in the morning," Ramsey says.

"Of course," I tell her. "My arm feels completely back to normal. My head is still pounding a bit, but that could just be from all of this." I wave my hand around in the air.

Ramsey chuckles. "It is likely the stress of learning all of this information or it could still be a side effect of using your power. But I can look to make sure that there isn't anything else going on. I also have some teas that you can take with you. Callum will know how to prepare them."

I nod my agreement. After we finish eating, I walk with Ramsey over to a comfortable seating area near the fireplace. "I should probably return your clothes," I say—not sure what else to talk about but needing to fill the silence somehow.

"Oh, god no. You can keep them. I put a bag with a couple more options in your room as well."

For some reason, I am an emotional wreck in this new world, and tears start to flood my eyes at her kindness. I quickly swipe them away. I can feel Cal watching me from across the room, so I quickly lock eyes with him and offer him a smile—letting him know that I am okay.

Sitting down, Ramsey explains how her magic works. Basically, it allows her to look inside my body like an xray, CT, and MRI. She can also use her magic to mend anything that needs it. Apparently, she was a nurse back in New York and has an eidetic memory. Those things combined with her magic have weaved themselves together into something incredible.

Her hands and eyes begin to glow silver, like moonlight, before she slowly pulls her magic back. "Everything looks how it should," she tells me.

After she tells me a bit more about herself and her sisters, we all say our goodbyes and head to our rooms for the night. They will be leaving in the morning to travel back to their family's lodge. As long as I am feeling up for travel, we will be leaving for Cal's keep as well.

"Ramsey told me that you have a little sister," I tell Cal as we get ready side by side for bed.

"Yes, I do. I thought that she had been killed along with the rest of my family until a few weeks ago. I traveled to meet with the Alphas to strengthen our alliance and found out that she was adopted by the Nightfury Alphas. She lives with them in their main village of Night."

"I would love to meet her sometime. I was an only child—raised by my grandmother. It sounds like we have that in common. And she has magic too?"

"Yes. Just like my grandmother, Juniper receives visions. If we were to have children one day, they may have visions like my line, or they may carry your power with them."

"And that is something that you want?" I ask crawling under the covers and scooching over enough for Cal to take up his spot next to me.

"Mo Chridhe, I want *everything* with you. But we can go at your pace. If that is never something that you want with me, I will be content to be there for you in whatever way you allow."

"Ramsey gave me some tea to prevent pregnancy. I know that we aren't at that point right now, but I am going to start drinking it."

"I will drink it too," he tells me.

And for some reason, the way that he doesn't question my desire to prevent pregnancy but to offer to take it too, means more to me than I thought possible. So, I give him another piece of me that I have not admitted to anyone before. Not even Sloane and Freya.

"I have always wanted children, but I never thought that I would be a good mother. My own mom abandoned me on my grandma's doorstep when I was just a baby. I'm not sure I would even know what to do."

Cal wraps his arm around my shoulders, tucking me up against him. "If children are in our future, I have no doubt that we will be able to figure it out together. We were destined to be partners in all aspects of life."

"Hey, Stud?" I ask, my voice turning a little gravelly. When he answers by giving me a smile, I continue. "I am going to need you to explain more about the whole Heart Mates thing—but can you just hold me tonight? I slept better last night than I have in years and I think it is because you were next to me."

"I will happily hold you every night for the rest of our lives," he admits as he pulls me down to rest my head on his chest. "Go to sleep, Mo Chridhe. I will be here when you wake."

"Stop!" I yell. Willing my nightmare to change into something else. I look over and see my friends laughing in the backseat of the town car. They don't know what will happen. They don't know that any second, a drunk driver is going to run a red light and barrel into us. But I see it all. My body is sitting there, looking exhausted after another long shift on my feet. But my eyes are looking down at the entire scene. And I know. I know that I am going to have to watch my friends die.

Refusing to look, I squeeze my eyes shut tight. "Please be okay. Please be okay," I chant as I hear the screech of tires. Just like that night, I move my body in between my friends. I do my best to shield them from danger. I am screaming for the car to stop, for us all to make it out of here alive. Nothing works. I cannot change what happened any more than I can change my dream. So, I brace myself for impact.

16
Honey

Callum

Her accelerated heartrate wakes me from my slumber. It takes me a few seconds to re-orient myself, but when I do, I immediately turn to my Mate. A golden light pulses from her chest, as if her magic is flowing from her Sun Kissed mark on her back, pushing through her body, and erupting in the space around us.

Heat envelops me, but it does not burn my skin. It glides over my skin like a loving caress, welcoming me into the safety of her magic even as she remains asleep.

There is a sheen of sweat on her brow and silent screams pour from her parted lips. She is having a nightmare.

"Wake, my love," I tell her softly as I brush my hand against her cheek. When she does not respond, I say it again a little louder.

Seconds after the golden light winks out, her eyes fly open and she gasps for air, clawing at my chest as if she desperately needs me to ground her back in this world. "You are safe, Mo Chridhe. It was only a dream," I whisper against her temple while I hold her tightly to my body. "I will not let anything hurt you."

"It felt so real," she admits, voice hoarse from the terror she witnessed.

"What happened?"

"It was the night before I woke up here." Her voice shakes despite her efforts to keep it even. "I was riding home from work with my friends. They never liked that I had to work so late at night so they would come in during my shift and wait to give me a ride home. It was all my fault." Willa shakes her head, frantically wiping the river of tears from her cheeks. "There was an accident. I didn't remember until I was talking to Ramsey earlier. We were riding in a car—a...um..machine that humans use for transportation. Another car hit ours. I saw it coming right before we collided. I threw my body over my friends—but there is no way they made it out of that crash unharmed. The car was moving too fast. It was so, so fast."

"And then you woke up by the lake?"

She nods her head, continuing to cry against my neck. We sit like that for so long, I think she may have fallen back to sleep.

"Cal?" Her voice is timid. Unsure. But still so brave. "Can you help me forget?"

Cupping her cheek in my hand, I maneuver us so that we are sharing a breath. I give her time to change her mind. But instead of pulling back away, she presses her lips to mine, licking her tongue at the seam, and then tangling her tongue with mine. The taste of her explodes on my tongue—the sweetest honey I have ever had, and I am desperate for more.

Angling her head to provide me with better access, I devour her. Rolling us, so that she is laying on her back with my body covering hers, I swallow her moans and press the hard ridge of my cock against her wet heat, and groan at the scent of her arousal.

"What do you need, my love?" I ask against her mouth before moving to leave a trail of hot kisses down her jaw, neck, and chest.

"I need you," she whines, rocking her hips up to grind against me and lifting her sleep shirt off her body.

Following her lead, I lower my head further and capture her taut nipple with my lips, sucking it into my mouth before biting down gently. She gasps but reaches up to hold me against her with one hand. Out of the corner of my eye, I watch as she teases her other nipple—twisting and pinching it with her fingers. I groan, seeing her play with herself sends a bolt of heat straight to my dick.

"Please, Cal," Willa moans as she applies gentle pressure to the top of my head, telling me that she is ready for me to move lower. I chuckle as I continue my descent, kissing, biting, and scraping my teeth against her delicate skin.

"Is this where you need me?" I ask, my mouth hovering so close to her center, she shivers as my breath breezes over her bare cunt.

Unable to help myself, I press in further, dragging my nose through her wet slit, and inhaling her orange blossom and honey scent. Now that she is completely turned on, her smell is even more intoxicating.

I dive in. Pressing my tongue firmly against her, I slowly drag it through her center, groaning as her taste bursts in my mouth. She is incredible. "I hope you are ready to let me drink your honey for every meal, Mo Chridhe."

"You can bathe in it as long as you keep going," she says as she grips my hair in her hand and holds my mouth to her cunt.

Laughing, I reach underneath her, spreading her as wide as possible before fucking my tongue in and out of her dripping center.

"Yes," she moans as she wets her fingers in her mouth before bringing them down to rub circles on her clit.

The sight of her taking her own pleasure in combination with her addictive taste causes me to shoot my seed all over the bed. But I don't let up. Reaching down to collect some of my cum, I bring my finger back up and slowly push it into her ass, marking her.

"Oh my god," she moans, riding my finger. I gently nudge her fingers away from her clit and replace them with my tongue before pulling that bundle of nerves into my mouth and sucking. Hard. She detonates, her body convulsing as her ass pulses around my finger and her pleasure pours into my waiting mouth.

When I return with a warm cloth to clean her up, she is still laying in the position that I left her in. "Are you okay?" I ask, hoping that it wasn't all too much for her.

"Am I okay?" She laughs. "Fuck, Stud. Why haven't we been doing *that* the entire time?"

I chuckle, pulling her back flush against my front, cradling her body with mine. Burying my head in her neck, I press my lips to her damp skin. "Go back to sleep, my love. Tomorrow we will travel home and I will properly worship you in our bed."

It isn't long before her breathing evens out and sleep claims us both.

17
The Prettiest Peen in the Bunch

Willa

The rising sun heats my face as I slowly stir awake. Rolling over, I stretch my arm across the mattress, seeking out the man who I know held me all night long. When my hand comes back empty, I open my eyes and find myself alone in bed. Where did he go?

Moments later, the door to our bedroom opens, spurring me to quickly cover my naked body with the blanket. When I realize it is Cal with a tray of food, I relax a little, but still feel more self-conscious in the light of day than I did last night.

"Good morning," he greets me with a smile. Setting the tray down on the side table, he leans in closer to give me a kiss. Turning my face so that his lips land on my cheek, he pulls away—his brows pinched together. "Is everything okay?" His words are full of concern.

"Good morning," I smile. "Everything is fine—just...morning breath."

Call growls. Full on growls, before climbing on top of me, straddling my hips, and leaning in to whisper in my ear. "There is nothing about you that could ever stop me from kissing you properly." I am so thrown off by his reaction that I do not twist my head when he dives in again, parting my lips with his tongue and kissing me so fiercely I can feel it in my toes. He swallows my moans greedily and it isn't long before I am squirming, trying to relieve some of the pressure that he is building between my legs.

He has my legs pinned so tightly together, I am unable to get any relief. "Please Cal," I beg.

Cal laughs. "I do love when you beg. But you will not come again until I let you. Consider it your punishment for trying to deny me your lips this morning."

"I'm sorry," I whine. "You can always have my lips. In fact, I insist. Start with these." I gesture to my pussy.

Cal's booming laughter fills the room as he crawls off of me. "Tempting, Mo Chridhe. Very tempting. But we don't have time for everything that I want to do to you."

"Then just pick one thing." Now that I am no longer pinned, I spread my legs wide, showing him exactly how needy I am for him. "Please kiss my pussy, Stud."

"Fuck," he whispers under his breath before pouncing—landing with his head right where I need him. "You are dripping, love. Is this all for me?"

"Mmhmm." His lips latch onto my clit, alternating between sucking and flicking me with his tongue, building me closer and closer to orgasm.

But, right before I am pushed over the edge, Cal pulls away, smirking, as he climbs back off of the bed. "Eat," he says. "We are leaving soon." He walks towards the door. "And if you finish what I started, you will be waiting even longer."

"Bad bear!" I shout as he howls with laughter and leaves me in a puddle of need.

Do I like his little punishment? Not one bit. However, my pussy is a traitorous little bitch who is practically panting for it. Realizing that he is not going to come back and finish the job, I make my way over to eat and then clean myself up for the day. I am not sure how far we need to travel, but it is already ridiculously hot out. Choosing the skimpiest, sheerest scraps of fabric that Ramsey brought me, I get dressed and head for the door. Two can play this game. If he wants to decide when I am allowed to come, I can decide that he needs to deal with my pussy dripping all over his back all day.

Several hours later, we stop for lunch near a stream. Bear Cal lowers himself to the ground, outstretching a leg so that I can more easily climb down. Determined to show him that I am not at all regretting my outfit for the day, I cover up my wince as I clumsily maneuver my body to slide off of his back.

I now understand the term "saddle sore" in a biblical sense.

Doing my best to move as normally as possible, I make my way over to the stream, stepping into the cool water.

This world really is beautiful. Giant trees, brightly covered leaves, and the clearest blue sky. And the air. I inhale it deeply into my lungs. The air is crisp and fresh despite the blistering sun. There is no place on Earth as pure as this. It is no wonder I was convinced that this was all a dream for so long.

Feeling eyes on my back, I slowly lower my hands into the water before bringing water up to splash on my heated skin. I look down and see that the water has also made the thin material of my top completely see through. Perfect.

Without turning around, I can feel Cal approaching. My heartbeat begins to accelerate, and I'm not sure who's heart is to blame.

I continue to let water slowly trickle down my skin, knowing that each bead of water has Cal's undivided attention. Taking a few more steps so that I am standing in knee-high water, I bend over, pushing my ass out, and spreading my legs just enough to know that he is seeing every inch of me through the thin, damp cloth.

A growl rumbles behind me. I have only seconds to prepare for impact before Cal's naked body crashes into mine and he rockets us both into the deepest part of the spring.

"You are a very naughty girl for teasing me today," he says in my ear before turning my head and devouring my mouth with his own.

Pulling back, breathless, I try to regain control. Fisting his large, hard, pierced cock in my hand, I tighten my grip and slowly drag my hand from root to tip. I really need to stop forgetting that his huge pipe has literal metal attached to it. I have never been with someone who was pierced before—but I am eager to feel how amazing it will be. "You are the one who denied me an orgasm this morning. Is my Mate regretting leaving me needy?"

His breath catches at my use of the word Mate and then his answering groan tells me that I have him right where I want him.

Turning my body so that his front is pressed to my back, I grind my ass on his rigid length—immediately regretting the action when a sharp, hot pain makes itself known. Fuck. My ass must be more irritated from riding on his back than I originally thought. Hearing my wince, Cal steps back, lowering to his knees behind me and lifting my skirt so that he can take a look.

"I'm so sorry, Mo Chridhe. Why didn't you tell me that you were injured?"

Feeling exposed, I swat his hand away, lowering my skirt and turning around to face him. "It just felt sore from riding. I didn't realize it was that irritated."

"I will hold you the rest of the way." His words are definitive. Not that I would protest anyway. I don't have any desire to irritate my skin further. Holding my hand, Cal walks with me out of the water, grabbing a small tin from Tor's pack. "This will help soothe your skin." He kneels behind me again, not noticing or caring that we now have an audience. The other men try to look busy, despite their quiet chuckles.

"Hey, Stud? Can we maybe do this somewhere else?"

He looks around our temporary camp before nodding and walking us over to one of the large trees away from the trail. "Next time you are injured, you will tell me right away," he grumbles, gently applying the ointment to my skin. I am pleasantly surprised to find out that the cream has a cooling effect and does not sting. "This should speed healing as well."

"I'm okay," I tell him. "I promise it isn't even that bad." He scoffs at my lie but doesn't call me out on it. "Will we make it to your keep tonight?"

"Yes. We should make it to *our* keep tonight. I sent a message ahead letting them know, so there should be dinner waiting for us."

Suddenly, I feel nervous. I *knew* that we would be traveling to his home. But I hadn't really put much thought into what that would mean for me. It isn't like I have any way of going back to Chicago. And, I really don't want to leave Cal, anyway. I still don't know what goes into being Heart Mates other than the freaky shared heartbeat thing—but since waking up in this world, it is clear that I have been forever changed. I get the feeling that if I were to separate from him for any real length of time, my heart would simply stop beating.

I should probably ask him. But there is something else on my mind while he helps me climb up onto Tor's back, settling me across his lap, adjusting me in such a way that my sore ass is not taking any of my weight. "Is there a reason for all of the...jewelry?"

Cal chuckles. "You noticed that, huh?"

"Your giant pierced cock is kind of hard to miss."

"Giant, you say?"

"Oh, shut up," I scold. "You know that is a massive trouser snake. I'm not even sure how you expect that thing to fit in me."

His laugh is louder now as he tips his face up to the sun. I can't help the smile that tugs at my lips. I love his laugh. He doesn't shy away from it or try to stifle it. There is something almost magical about it.

"You will take my cock into your body like a good girl, and I promise you will enjoy it."

A whimper leaves my lips as I squeeze my legs together. The mouth on this man. Have I ever been a 'good girl' type of girl before? Nope. Am I ready to tattoo 'Cal's Good Girl' across my chest? Maybe.

Cal takes a deep breath and then rumbles a pleased growl. The answering snarl from Bear Tor reminds me that this is definitely not the time to be getting so worked up.

"Relax, cousin," Cal tells him. "We aren't going to fuck on your back in the middle of the forest."

Bear Tor chuffs and picks up his pace, making Cal and I both laugh.

"You were asking about my jewelry," Cal reminds me.

"Yes. Um. Is it a bear thing or a you thing?"

"Both," he explains. "As you know, the Sun Kissed magic is carried on in my family line. While males in my line can pass the magic on to the next generation, we do not receive a Sun Kissed mark." He trails his fingers over the mark on my back. "But as a sign of our lineage, Sun Kissed males go through a ritual, marking our bodies with the gold that represents our line. For bears, gold can only be worn by the Sun Kissed. It is one of the reasons why our families were targeted by the rebel clans. Greed for our gold, as well as our land, prestige, and power."

"And the other guys in your clan don't carry on the magic, so they don't have the same adornments?"

"Have you been looking at the cocks of other males?" he teases.

"No!" I quickly deny. "But when you are all standing around naked after shifting, it is glaringly obvious that you have the prettiest peen in the bunch." Truthfully, I haven't seen them all—but the ones that I have caught a glimpse of have been gold free.

Cal's roar of laughter is accompanied by chuffs from all four bears in our groups. Apparently, they aren't even going to pretend to give us privacy anymore.

I smile, happy that at least some of his clan are warming up to me.

18
A Big Deal

Callum

Willa gasps the moment the keep comes into view.

The sound hits me square in the chest.

She's told me about her world—about concrete and steel and buildings stacked atop one another like they're competing for space. I try to imagine her reaction now, seeing my family's forest-bound stronghold rising from the land like it was grown instead of built. Stone softened by moss. Towers woven through ancient trees. Home.

"Cal," she says, lightly smacking my shoulder, though her eyes never leave the keep. "You could have mentioned that you're a big deal."

I huff out a laugh, though pride and unease twist together inside me. "I'll show you just how big of a deal I am once we get you into our bed, my love. But first," I add, sobering, "there are people we need to see."

That's the part for which I didn't fully prepare her. Or myself, if I'm honest.

I did send word ahead that I was returning. I just…omitted a crucial detail. I did not inform them that I found my Heart Mate. I did not mention that she is human. My close friends notwithstanding, bears are traditional. A lot of weight is put on following what has been done in the past. Rituals that need to happen. Pairings that are considered suitable. And throwing a human into the mix? That is sure to put many into a frenzy.

Perhaps I should have gone about informing my clan differently, but in reality, there is nothing that they can do to change fate. Our bond, though not yet sealed, is already locked into my bones so deeply that the thought of anyone challenging it makes my bear restless beneath my skin.

We cause a stir the moment Tor approaches the gates with us on his back. I can feel the shift—heads turning, magic stirring, curiosity sharpening into something more dangerous. Gossip will race through the keep faster than fire through dry brush. My aunt will know before I've even dismounted.

Which is why we will face her tonight.

Tor crouches once we're inside the gates, extending his leg. I slide down, holding Willa securely against my chest. When my feet touch the ground, she wiggles for freedom, but I only loosen my hold enough to set her down, my arm stays firm around her waist as we stride toward the opening doors.

"Ready?" I murmur, my lips brushing her ear.

She shakes her head immediately. "No. I'm really nervous, Cal. What if they don't want me here?"

The question slices deeper than she realizes.

I stop us, turn her fully into my arms, and tip her chin up so she has no choice but to look at me. "You are my Heart Mate," I say quietly. "The most sacred bond that exists. This is my family's home—and therefore, it is yours."

Her eyes shine but doubt still trembles in her voice. "Just because you want me here doesn't mean they will. Won't they be upset that I'm not a bear?"

I should have told her sooner. I should have armored her with truth instead of assuming my authority would be enough.

I pull her closer, lowering my mouth to her ear. Others will hear, being in such close proximity, but they will know these words are meant only for her.

"I don't often speak of it because I don't *feel* different from my clan," I say. "But I am Clan Chief. This is your home because I say it is. Others are here because I allow it.

Anyone who disrespects you will lose my favor." My voice hardens. "It does not matter to me that you are not a bear. You are Sun Kissed. Your magic could reshape this world."

I pause, pressing a kiss to her temple.

"And if you woke tomorrow without that mark, without magic at all, I would still choose you. Every time. Because you are *mine*."

She exhales slowly, nodding, her fingers weaving through mine. "Okay. Let's get this over with."

The sitting room is full.

Too full.

At least twenty sets of eyes snap toward us as we enter. I hadn't expected a welcoming party at this hour, but we've been gone for weeks, and my absence always breeds unrest. I feel Willa tense immediately as she tries to hide behind me. I move her to stand in front of me, banding my arm around her waist, and silently declaring our relationship for all to see.

They don't bow.

I stop.

Silence stretches until Tor clears his throat behind us. Instantly, bodies drop. Heads bowed, knees bent, voices offering greeting.

All except my aunt.

Aurora stands tall, wearing her best dress as if this is some kind of formal event despite the late hour and my cadre and I dressed in equal parts wrinkled trousers and dirt from weeks of travel.

The rest of the clan is dressed in various stages of casual attire. Much more akin to what I would expect, making Aurora's outfit and insolence stand out even more.

Normally, I don't care. Tonight, it grates. She should be bowing to my Mate.

I shake off the irritation and kiss Willa's shoulder before addressing the room. "I know there are matters that require attention, but they will wait until morning."

They don't like it. I can feel it. But I don't care.

Willa's heartbeat had gone frantic, fluttering against my chest like a trapped bird. She's overwhelmed. That makes this simple.

I guide her toward the buffet, keeping my body angled protectively as I fix her a plate. The stares burn into my back. She presses closer, trusting me to handle what she cannot yet face.

Once we're in the hall, alone, she finally breathes.

"Are you okay?" I ask.

She lets out a shaky laugh. "I used to have this nightmare where I'd show up to something important in my underwear. Everyone would laugh and I would run away crying." She gestures towards the now closed door. "That felt similar. I hadn't thought about the possibility of meeting so many people when I chose this outfit to torture you this morning."

I set the tray aside and pull her into my arms. "You are beautiful in any state of dress," I murmur. "They stared because I failed to warn them. That's on me."

She nods, then asks softly. "Was that your aunt? Waterboy's mom?"

"Yes," I chuckle. "Aurora. My mother's sister."

"What was your mother's name?"

"Dawn." Saying it feels like a quiet offering. A memory I don't share lightly.

"That is a pretty name. I wish I could have met her. And your grandmother—the one who saved your sister. I wish I could have met her too."

"Me too, Mo Chridhe." After a few long minutes of holding her in the hallway, Willa takes a deep breath. Grabbing my hand, she allows me to retrieve our forgotten dinner before continuing in the direction of our quarters.
"I don't think she likes me. Aurora. Her eyes were shooting daggers at me," she says quietly.

I was hoping that she hadn't noticed my aunt's lack of respect. "I think she was just surprised. I have never been one to bring a female into the keep." She nods her head, though she still looks uncertain. "Let's eat and then we can go to bed. It has been a long day."

Before the rebels burned through the territory, the keep housed my family, guests, and staff. Other clan members had their own homes in the area. However, now that there are so few of us left and the rebels continue to attack, I have moved my entire clan into my home. There is plenty of room for all of us, but it does make it more difficult to separate my personal life from my role as Clan Chief. It is a double-edged blade, making it easier for my clan to see me and discuss issues, but it also makes it easier for my clan to impose on my personal life. It is one of the reasons why I was so adamant about keeping my personal quarters separate from everyone else that now calls the keep home.

I'm so caught in thoughts of tomorrow—of council, of war, of my aunt's obvious displeasure—that I don't sense the wrongness until Willa gasps.

"There you are," a female voice purrs.

My bear surges.

A growl tears from my chest as fury detonates through me. My entire body shakes as I struggle to remain in control of my bear.

"Tor!" I roar, knowing that he will be able to hear me from his chambers.

Next to me, Willa is breathing erratically. Our hearts beat in a wild rhythm that is caused by equal parts rage and confusion. I force a breath, trying to prevent my anger from overwhelming her system.

Moments later, Tor bursts through the door, half dressed, and ready to provide backup despite not knowing what situation he just walked into.

"Remove this female from the keep and then retrieve your mother," I command. He sucks in a breath, realizing the severity of the situation, but quickly schools his face and drags the naked female from my bed, ignoring her protests, and leaves the room.

Reaching out to pull the cord next to the door and wait for my staff to answer the call. Willa hasn't said anything, but I can still feel her racing heart. I band my arms tightly around her, pulling her chest to mine. She buries her face into my neck but remains silent.

When a staff member knocks on the door, I instruct them to change all the bedding so that the woman's scent is removed from our room. Once they leave, Willa finally speaks.

"Who was that?" she asks, her voice shaky.

"I do not know," I tell her honestly. "She is not a member of my clan."

"Why was she here?" she asks, sounding even more confused. My heart splinters at the uncertainty she is feeling—at the doubt in her mind that I might have invited another woman into my bed.

"That is what I intend to find out," I tell her. "I do not know for certain, but I believe my aunt is behind this. It isn't the first time she has done something like this. I have let her behavior go on for long enough."

"What are you going to do?"

Before I have a chance to answer her, Tor returns with Aurora in tow. "You wanted to see me?" she asks, feigning innocence. It is all too much.

"Would you like to explain why there was an unknown female left naked in our bed tonight?" I ask.

"I do not know what you are talking about," she states firmly. Tor tenses at her side, knowing that she just sealed her own fate.

"You dare lie to my face?" I snarl, no longer forcing my bear back as we take a protective step in front of our Mate.

"I just thought you might want company after your journey. I did not know that you were bringing your own plaything." She clucks her tongue at Tor as he shakes his head and takes a step away from her.

"Willa is *not* my *plaything,*" I roar. "She is my Heart Mate. My fated. Mine!"

Willa's small hand curls around my arm, a gentle reminder of her presence and need for me to stay in control.

"You will move out of your quarters and into the staff wing," I say, my voice low but firm. "You will rise with our cook each morning and take direction from the staff. You will no longer be privy to clan meetings and will earn a wage based on your new duties. Do you understand?"

Instead of answering me, she turns her attention to her son. "Torin, you cannot let him do this to me!"

Tor lifts his head to meet her gaze. "Cal is our Chief," he tells her.

"But we are family!" she yells.

"Family does not know the blatant disrespect that you have shown tonight," I state. "Are you so blinded by your own desires that you fail to see what is standing right in front of you? You have always wished for me to find a Mate. To settle down and further our line. I have found her, Aurora. I have found the female who makes my heart sing."

"How could she possibly be your Heart Mate when she doesn't even have a bear?" she sneers. "She is one of those *humans*, isn't she?" She spits the word "humans" as if it burns her tongue on the way out.

Stepping around me, Willa positions herself so that her back is pressed against my front. "Yes," she says. "I am human. I do not know how I came to be here, but the fact remains that I am. And I *am* Cal's Heart Mate. I might not fully understand what that means yet—this world and everything in it are foreign to me—but I can tell you with absolute certainty that he will not choose another. In the short time that we have known each other, he has sunk beneath my skin, burrowed himself in my bones, and has made himself a home in my heart. *You* might not like or accept me as I am—but *he* does. And that is the only thing that matters to me."

Aurora stands shocked still. She might not be used to taking commands, but she certainly understands the authority that was just shown to her. "Staff will already be clearing out your bedchamber and moving your belongings into your new room. I suggest you go and help them. That will be all for tonight," I say, dismissing her. Tor gives me a subtle nod in thanks, knowing that his mother's punishment could have been much worse, before leading her out of the room.

As soon as the door snicks closed, Willa spins to face me. Her heavy breaths, her pulse, her pink-tinged cheeks, are all signs of the adrenalin pumping through her blood. And when she tips her head back, locking her glittering eyes with mine, she has never looked more beautiful.

"I could drown in your depths," I tell her, tucking a wild strand of her midnight hair behind her ear. "I wouldn't kick my feet or try to claw myself to the surface. I would let your essence swirl around me in a ferocious wave and never once ask to breathe."

"Cal?"

"Yes, Mo Chridhe?"

"Take me to bed."

19
Count

Willa

Cal wastes no time, gripping my thighs and lifting me, my legs instinctively wrapping around his waist as he presses his hardening cock against my core. I gasp, feeling the length of him and knowing without a doubt that I have never been with someone so well endowed.

Walking us over to our freshly made bed, Cal lowers me onto my back, crawling over me and settling his large body between my thighs. "You are so fucking beautiful," he tells me, pressing kisses to my jaw and neck.

"I need you inside me," I tell him, pawing unsuccessfully at our clothes. Cal chuckles at my failed attempts before taking over, not stopping until we are both completely bare.

"Are you too sore?" he asks, reminding me that I do, in fact, have a raw ass from riding on his back earlier in the day.

Am I sore? Yes. Is it going to stop me from what is likely going to be the best orgasm of my life? Absolutely not. If I tell him that my ass still hurts, he is going to insist we wait and I am far too needy for that to happen. Reaching down between my legs, I dip my finger into my center before raising it to his lips. Without breaking eye contact, he wraps his lips around my glistening finger, sucking it into his mouth and moaning at the taste.

"I need you to fuck my pussy. That is the *only* thing that will help relieve this ache." Taking his studded cock in my hands, I swipe the drop of pre-cum from the tip with my thumb to have a taste before lining him up with my entrance. "Please," I whimper.

"I love hearing you beg," he growls before pushing the head of his cock into my body and crashing his lips to mine in a way that is sure to bruise. Moving to my jaw, he drags his teeth against my skin on the way to my ear. "Count."

My moment of confusion soon becomes clear as he pushes his cock further into me, the first piercing rubbing against me on its way in. "One," I rasp out right before he pushes in further, his next piercing dragging against my walls as they stretch to accommodate his size. "Two," I moan.

A satisfied rumble comes from Cal's chest as he lowers his mouth to my peaked nipple, flicking the bud with his tongue before gently biting down on it.

"Three," I pant as he fills me further, going so slow that even the slightest movement is felt. I twine my fingers in his hair and force his mouth back up to mine, tangling my tongue with his while he tortures me with his cock.

"Four," I say against his lips.

"Five," I yelp as he returns to my nipple and bites down hard.

"Halfway there, Mo Chridhe. You are taking me so well," he says against my breast.

Halfway? I am already so full, but I know I will not be satisfied until I have every single inch slicked in my wet heat.

"Please," I whine, grabbing his delicious ass with my hands and pressing him closer to me. Another rumble fills the air. I am certain that he is going to continue this slow torture, but he surprises me by pulling my ear lobe into his mouth and growling, "Say ten."

"Ten!" I shout as he slams the rest of his cock into me, hitting me so deep, I can feel it pulse against my heart. His thrusts are hard and steady, building my orgasm so high, I'm not sure I will ever come back down. He is in me so deep—

mind, body, and soul—I know that I will never be the same. Cal kisses me, thrusting his tongue into my mouth in time with his cock.

Moments before completely giving myself over to the wave that is cresting, I remember something about Cal—something that I know will make him feral with need for me—so I momentarily break our kiss and ask the three word question that I know he is dying to hear, even if he hasn't demanded it yet.

"Can I come?"

"Fuuuuuuuck," he moans, reacting just as I knew he would. "Come for me, my love. Take your pleasure and my seed. It all belongs to you."

I recapture his mouth with mine, sucking his tongue into my mouth and working it over like I would if it was his cock instead. His thrusts become harder, more erratic. The piercing that he has at the base of his cock rubs perfectly against my clit, sending me soaring. Wave after wave of pleasure crashes over me as he finds his own release and fills me with hot ropes of cum. Still inside, he rolls us so that I am spread out on top of him while we both catch our breath.

"That was…" I start, unable to finish my thought with my two functioning brain cells.

"Fucking perfect," Cal agrees.

Too blissed out to function, I give in to my more primal side and bury my face into his neck, inhaling his amazing scent. He smells like home in a way that I have never experienced before. I want to bottle it up so that I never need to live without it again.

I try to form words—to tell him what he means to me—but my brain and my tongue are malfunctioning. "I think you broke my brain with your giant bedazzled dick," I mumble, causing him to roar with laughter.

"Admittedly, I do not know much about human anatomy—though what I have discovered so far is flawless—but I am pretty sure that even my giant dick cannot reach your brain from your...what do humans call it? Oh yeah. Your pussy."

"You aren't giving yourself enough credit," I chuckle. "With all that metal, that is a literal weapon you are packing."

Cal snorts a laugh. "I promise he is a lover, not a fighter."

"I did get that impression, yes." I giggle as he reaches his hand around to tickle me. My stomach chooses that moment to growl, reminding us both of the forgotten food across the room. Slipping free, Cal settles me under the covers before retrieving our tray.

"Eat," he commands. I hold back my comment about not taking orders from anyone, knowing that his abruptness is due to his instincts needing me to be taken care of.

"Eat with me," I say, patting the mattress next to where I sit. He does not hesitate to climb back into bed, pressing his thigh against mine and pulling the tray so that it sits across his lap.

"I'm sorry about my aunt," he tells me quietly. "I wish I could say that this is the first time she has tried something like that—but I can't. Anytime that there is a bonding sun, she tries to persuade me into taking a mate by leaving them in my bed."

I scoff, not at Cal's admission but at the idea that his aunt would try to force his hand like that.

"At first," he continues, "I could avoid them by hiding out somewhere else in the keep. But, after time, they were instructed to seek me out. It got to the point where I would just leave altogether."

"And you didn't want to settle down?"

"No. I have always wanted a partner. But not just anyone. I wanted my Heart Mate." Cal takes a moment, smiling to himself as he gathers his thoughts. "Sun Kissed receive their mark on their 5th birthday—but only the females in the line can bear the mark. When I was a little boy, I wanted so badly to receive a mark but knew that it would never come. Like my sister, Juni, my Nana was a daydreamer—she had visions of the future—and she told me that one day, my heart would sing. Over the years, I thought that it was possible that she was just trying to make me feel better. But I still held out hope that my Heart Mate—that you—would be found."

"And now your heart sings?"

"Yes. It beats for you. Only ever for you."

"I can feel it," I tell him, raising his hand to my chest. "Mine beats for you too. I think it always has."

Raising his hand to my face, he gently cradles my jaw and tips my head back before pressing his lips to mine in a tender kiss.

"Back in my world, I had a heart condition," I explain. "The doctors called it a congenital heart defect, but their tests never actually showed a malformation or physical defect. When I was little, my lips would turn blue, I would tire easily, and my heartbeats were irregular. I learned ways to manage it, to reduce overworking my heart, but the cause remained unknown. When I woke up in this world, I felt my heart stutter before finding a new rhythm. Our rhythm. I think…is it crazy to think that my heart knew that I was supposed to be here all along?"

Cal wraps his arm around me, tucking me close to his chest. "That isn't crazy at all. I *know* that you were always meant to be here, with me." Looking into his eyes, I can feel the truth behind his words.

"Tomorrow, I am going to need you to tell me more about this whole Heart Mates and bonding sun thing. But right now, I think we should get some sleep."

I excuse myself to use the bathroom and get ready for bed. I debate putting on a nightshirt but decide that I would much rather feel Cal's skin on mine, so I climb back into my cozy spot tucked up next to Cal's side. His arm comes back around me, holding me close.

"Goodnight, Stud," I say with a yawn.

"Sleep well, my love," he says as he presses a kiss to my forehead. And then, right as I am about to let sleep take me, his low voice fills the air, singing a soul-stirring lullaby. The words are foreign to me, but the love that he pours into the song wraps around my heart as a promise for all that we are and all that we will become.

20
Sex Dungeons & Stalemates

Callum

The sun peeks in through the drawn curtains, casting the room in a soft golden glow. This has always been my favorite time of the day—right before the world wakes, ready to start anew. This morning is made perfect with my Mate pressed against me, skin slicked with sweat from our shared body heat, the scent of my cum still marking her as *mine*.

Despite our late arrival last night, there will already be members awaiting me in the meeting room, ready to give me updates about the rebel uprising. Rumors will have spread about Aurora's punishment. And there will be a swarm of questions about Willa and the role that she will take on. But I do not want to leave my bed.

Here, the world is quiet.

Here, I know that my Mate is safe from warring clans and meddlesome busybodies.

Here, I can just be me. Not someone who is responsible for many. Not someone who needs to further the Sun Kissed line. Not Clan Chief—just Callum.

But the world does not remain still for long. Shouting in the hallway has pulled my attention away from the way that the sunlight glints off the soft curve of Willa's cheekbone and has forced me into action.

Gently removing myself from underneath Willa, I pull on a pair of leather pants and, with one last look at her sleeping form, I leave my Mate to sleep soundly in our bed.

"You can't just go barging in there," Bo growls from outside my door. I do not typically have a guard standing watch in my quarters, but with all of the commotion that last night brought on, I'm sure Tor arranged for the extra security.

"I'm not 'barging in,'" Aurora snarls. "I am now a housemaid, haven't you heard? Demoted for caring too much."

Not wanting to have this conversation so soon after waking but knowing that I have no choice, I scrub my hand over my face before opening the door just enough to slip outside.

"Is there something that you need?" I ask my aunt, not bothering to mask my annoyance.

"What I need is for you to stop this nonsense and let me return to my room. My *actual* room. I simply cannot be made to sleep with the servants! Did you know that they are up at all hours of the night, coming and going, not to mention partaking in carnal activities long into the night?"

I can't help the laugh that bursts from my lungs at the idea of my 200-year-old aunt being scandalized by *carnal activities*. "Surely it isn't anything you haven't been witness to before," I tell her. "I know for a fact that you have walked in on your own son deep in the throes of pleasure. And you do, indeed, have a son, which tells me that you are not so virginal yourself."

Aurora's cheeks flame beet red while she gasps and covers her mouth with her hand. Next to me, Bo can no longer stifle his reaction and explodes with laughter. I can't blame him.

"The staff quarters, while smaller than what you are accustomed to, are not a sex dungeon. You have a private bedchamber as well as your own bathing space. The staff come and go at all hours of the night because they are doing their jobs—receiving deliveries, cleaning spaces, and answering calls from other members who live in this house—which, up until last night, included you. Did you think that your nightly tea and brandy just appeared each night? That the scones that you enjoy each morning make themselves? Our staff are more important to this keep than many of its other inhabitants and you *will* show them the respect that you lacked to show my Mate and me last night. Do you understand?"

Aurora scoffs before answering my question with a low, "yes."

"Great! Now, if you will excuse me, I am going to go and wake my Mate up with my tongue. You can spread the word that we are not to be disturbed at this early hour unless the world is on fire." With a quick look to Bo, I slip back into my room and do just that.

"Are you sure they are going to be okay with me crashing this meeting?" Willa asks as we make our way towards the large gathering room, where at least half of the clan is currently awaiting us.

"I am the Clan Chief and you are my Heart Mate. You are not crashing anything. We are equal."

"But I don't know the first thing about what is going on," she replies, clearly nervous with how she whisper-shouts at me.

"That is why it is doubly important that you are there with me. And, you know more than you might think. You were there for more than one attack. Many of my clan members have not seen the conflict that close, remaining in the safety of the keep."

"But what if…" she shakes her head. "Never mind."

Stopping in the middle of the hallway, I wrap Willa up into my arms. "Please tell me."

"What if they don't like me? I don't usually care what others think about me. Back in Chicago, I let things just roll off of my shoulders. I was pretty confident. Even when I was struggling to make ends meet, I was still sure about who I was and what I was capable of. But here, I don't know. It's like I'm off kilter. I have all of this magic buzzing inside of me and I do not know how to use it, I don't even know where to begin, but I know that this is where I belong. With you, I feel like I can be myself—even more than I ever have in my entire life. But with everyone else, I just feel like I am not going to be enough."

I rub her back in soothing circles as she puts words to all of her feelings and lets them out into the world. She has been so brave. I know that this world is vastly different from the one that she is from, but she has taken every new change in stride. I can't imagine what it must feel like for her to be displaced so abruptly.

"I'm sorry," she continues. "I know that this isn't the time for me to spiral."

"You do not need to apologize. Never to me. Never for this." I gently grasp her chin with my fingers, tilting her gaze to mine. "I think that it is understandable that you are feeling a little out of sorts. We will figure out your magic together. Tor is already doing some research to see if anyone in our history has developed a similar power. He is also sending messages out to the other surviving Sun Kissed Clan Chiefs to discuss the prophecy and what it all means going forward. But most importantly, please know that you are more than enough. To me, you are everything."

Willa pushes up on her toes, holding my cheek in her small hand, before pressing her lips to mine. Wanting to reassure her, I deepen the kiss and pour my heart out into it, swallowing her air along with her fears, and replacing them with my certainty. She kisses me back just as fiercely, getting lost in the feel of her body pressed to mine. It isn't until Bo clears his throat that we break apart breathless.

"Are you ready?" I ask, tipping my forehead against hers, still sharing the air between us.

With a nod, she takes my hand and takes a half step away from me. Her cheeks tinge pink when she realizes that we are not alone in this hallway. Bo and Colt stand at our backs, ready to provide any aid that we might need. I doubt we are in any actual danger going into this meeting, but bears are known to run hot and tempers can quickly flair.

Entering the room, I take note of everyone who is waiting for us as I walk Willa across the room to where the breakfast buffet is set up, selecting a variety of foods for us to share while we hear the clan's concerns. Almost everybody is seated at the long table that takes up the bulk of the room. Apart from my seat at the head of the table, all other chairs have been taken—including the one that my aunt typically occupies.

Pulling my chair away from the table so that she can more easily sit, I help Willa into my seat, propping myself on the arm of the chair. Everyone in the room, besides my cadre, are shocked. Some do a better job at hiding it than others, though. I make note of all of their reactions, still not believing that any of them would cause a real issue, but in the times that we live in, you can never be too cautious.

"Good morning," I say to break the shocked silence.

Willa, to my amusement, has paid no outward attention to the others at the table. She is not oblivious to the awkwardness but focuses instead on eating her breakfast as if this is something that she does every single day. When I receive no reply from my clan, she lifts her fork to my mouth. "I think you broke them, Stud. You might as well eat while their brains catch up."

Tor, Bo, and Colt all snicker. I can't blame them. It is taking much of my concentration to not break out in laughter myself. Who knew that a change in the seating arrangement would disable so many bears.

"Any updates?" I ask the room, unsure who will snap free from whatever hold my Mate has on them first.

"I have dispatched the messages that we discussed," Tor confirms.

"And I have spoken with the patrols. The rebels are encroaching like we predicted, but there are many more of them than we guessed," Bo adds.

"Double our overnight guards—create two lines of defense. If they attack, they will do it under the cover of night," I command. "Anyone else?" I look around the table where most have quietly gone back to eating without offering up any information or issues. "Surely there is a reason why you are all here—is there another issue that needs my attention?"

Arturas, Colt's father, clears his throat. "I could not help but notice that Aurora is not here."

I wait for him to continue, but he remains quiet. "Good to know your vision still works. Was there a question associated with that observation?" Next to me, Willa's head tilts down as she stifles a laugh. My words were laced with more snark than I would typically employ, but holding court is one of my least favorite responsibilities and I would much rather be dealing with real issues than having to explain myself for a punishment that was rightfully earned.

"Will we be seeing her again anytime soon?"

"Yes, I'm sure you will. She should be spending her days working throughout the keep and it is likely that you will cross paths. But that isn't what you meant to ask, was it? Just so we are clear, I do not owe any of you an explanation. However, my Mate has elevated my mood significantly this morning and I am feeling generous. Aurora overstepped and made a grave mistake in being disrespectful instead of remorseful. Cook needed help in the kitchens, so that is where she now serves."

Arturas scoffs, confirming my suspicions that their relationship has grown beyond friendship. "I'm sure she didn't intend..."

"Stop," I say, holding up my hand. "Despite your faith in her intentions, she absolutely meant what she said and did. Aurora is a highly intelligent individual—what she didn't think would happen was for me to bestow the punishment that she has deserved for quite some time."

"Whatever she did, it could not have been so bad that she needs to work in the kitchens," he argues on her behalf.

I have reached my limit with this conversation, and am about to say so, when Willa stands abruptly. "Do any of you have Heart Mates?" she asks. About half of the room signals that they do, in fact, have Heart Mates. Willa nods, looking each of them in the eye before she continues. "What would the appropriate punishment have been if someone forced a naked woman into your bedchamber, acting as if *you* were the one to leave them there waiting, just so that your Heart Mate could discover her? And then, when confronted about it, that person lied to your face, only to later confess that she was providing a more suitable *plaything* than the Heart Mate that you have brought home?"

Faces pale and anger rises. Not towards my Mate, but *for* her. Everyone but Arturas.

"She wouldn't have..." he starts.

"She did," Tor states firmly. "I was witness to it all."

"Now, I am new to this world," Willa continues, "but I am told that the punishment for disrespect such as this is usually more severe than being moved to a slightly smaller, but still private room and needing to contribute to the maintenance of such a large residence. Would you like us to adjust her sentence to more fairly reflect her actions?"

My heart swells with pride. She was worried about not fitting in—not being enough—but she just commanded the room with the grace of a queen. She is so much more than I could have ever hoped for.

"No? Great." Willa sits back down and lifts her plate into my hands. "More sausage, please." Tor, Bo, and Colt have smiles that match my own.

But they aren't the only ones.

She has just won over the respect of the clan.

21
Drop It Like It's... A Lot

Willa

A moan leaves my lips as Cal's tongue dives deep into my center.

After our little standoff with Arturas, a portly man with thinning hair and a handlebar mustache—I am truly baffled how he shares genes with the tall glass of water that is his son, Colt—the conversation at the table became productive. Clan members gave Cal updates on all attacks that occurred in the area while he was away as well as movements towards the keep by rebel clans.

Cal updated everyone on the attacks that we experienced as well, though he did leave out the details of my aid in those skirmishes. I trust him to choose the right time to let them know that I have the ability to blast enemies away with my magic. Magic that I have no idea how to control or use purposefully.

After the updates were given and tasks were divided up, Cal dismissed everyone from the room before swiping the table clear and positioning me on the edge, giving him full and easy access to the meal he has been craving for the last hour—his words, not mine.

Edging me with his dirty mouth, Cal brings me so close to the release I need but never lets me quite get there. He is doing it on purpose, and my pussy is acting as if she is totally fine with this never-ending climb to the top, even if it doesn't lead to the mind-blowing orgasm that would send us flying.

"You taste so fucking sweet," he says against my skin, pulling away only long enough to bite my thigh and spear his thick fingers into my pussy.

Diving back in, he scrapes his tooth against my clit, causing me to cry out and spasm around his fingers. His expert touch and the idea that anyone could walk in on us has me, once again, soaring so close to the edge, I can't take it any longer. I *need* to come more than I have needed anything. "Please, Cal."

He lets out a pleased growl before standing and pulling his fingers free. I whimper at the loss of him. "The last time you said 'please,' you were asking for more sausage." He chuckles. "You asked so nicely, I couldn't possibly deny you." Seconds later, Cal has worked himself free from his pants and thrusts every inch of his studded cock inside me in one hard motion.

I scream, not caring who can hear me, as an orgasm rips through me.

Mumbling something that I don't understand, Cal removes himself and rips my dress down the center, leaving me completely bare, star-fished on the table, before bringing his hand down in a quick slap to my pussy.

I open my mouth to protest but then he administers another quick smack and my traitorous pussy weeps for more. Moaning instead of scolding, it is clear that I no longer have any control over my body or my reactions to this man.

Leaning over me, he bites my ear before whispering, "Next time, you will ask before you come all over my cock."

I know that he isn't actually angry, but his words burst the euphoric bubble I was floating in. I can't help but think that he is disappointed in me. Or that I did something wrong. "I'm sorry," I sob, suddenly aware of the tears in my eyes right before they fall.

Before I know what is happening, Cal has me cradled in his arms. I cling to him, allowing him to comfort me as a tidal wave of emotions completely takes over. "I don't know what is happening," I quietly admit, pressing my face into his neck.

"I'm so sorry, Mo Chridhe. I went too far."

I can see the remorse in his eyes. But even more, I can *feel* it in his heart. I don't know how to describe it, but just like how our hearts beat in time with each other, the more time that I have spent with Cal, the clearer it is to feel what he feels.

"You didn't do anything wrong," I assure him, even though my tears keep flowing. "I really liked all of that. I don't know why I am crying."

I shiver in his arms despite my body feeling like it is on fire. Am I sick?

"You aren't sick, my love. This can happen sometimes. We should have discussed all of this before, but I got carried away." Cal loosens his grip on me long enough to slip his shirt over my head; I snuggle back into the warmth of his hold. "I'm here, sweetheart. You are safe with me."

I don't know how long we sit like that, with Cal holding me and the steady beat of our hearts slowly returning to a normal rhythm. Eventually, we make it back to our room, where Cal lowers me into the bathtub, adding oils to the hot water, before climbing in behind me and returning me to his arms.

"This feels nice," I tell him, feeling exhausted but more comfortable than I have in a while. Nobody has ever taken care of me like this before.

Not that I would have let them.

I was always determined to do things for myself—all alone. It is part of the reason why finding all of those unpaid bills and loans that my grandmother had hidden away in a drawer completely derailed my life. It wasn't simply that I needed to find a job to keep the house. That was part of it. But I could have easily asked for help from my friends and then continued with school, paying them back once I had the career that I dreamed of for so long. The thing that *really* threw me off was that she had made all of those sacrifices, and I didn't even know. I never got to tell her how much it meant to me. I wasted so much time reaching for the next best thing, that I did not stop to notice the truth of how I was able to get there in the first place.

Probably sensing the inner spiral that has wrapped around my heart, Cal holds me a little tighter. "Are you okay?"

I nod. "I think everything just caught up to me. I'm sorry that I reacted that way. I'm..." Embarrassed. Grieving. Overwhelmed.

"You do not need to apologize."

I turn around, straddling his lap and bringing my pruney fingers up to his face. "Please promise me that you will try again. All of it. I... I want to do it all again."

He opens his mouth to reply, but I bring my finger to his lips, cutting him off—already knowing that he is going to tell me that we don't have to.

"Before coming here, I went through life wanting to prove myself as the best. The best student. The best athlete. The best debater. The best at everything. And with that, came the need to control. Control the environment around me. Control the relationships I was in. It bled into every aspect of my life. But with you, I don't need to. I can just be me. The real, stripped-down version of me. My friends, Freya and Sloane, got close—but even with them, I hid parts of myself. I couldn't ask for help. I *knew* that I could trust them with anything, but I still didn't offer everything up to them."

"It's different with me," he states. It isn't a question because he can feel it too. The truth of it blazing in our shared heart.

I nod. "With you, I can let go. I know that I am safe. I know that even if I am not the best, you won't see me any differently. So try again. Okay?"

Cal drops his forehead to mine before taking my lips in a kiss so gentle, I can feel his care for me deep in my bones. "Okay," he whispers against my lips. "But not tonight. You need to rest."

I nod, knowing that he isn't going to budge on this. And, I do feel completely wiped out, exhausted from my outpouring of emotions.

"Wake up, my love." Cal's voice cuts through the dreamy fog I was lost in, pulling me back to the surface. Peeking an eye open, I notice that it is dark out. I must have slept the rest of the day away.

"What time is it?" I ask, still slightly confused.

"It is nearly dinner time," he tells me. "I was going to let you keep sleeping, but your stomach has been growling and I couldn't bear it."

"That's okay," I tell him. "I'm sorry that I slept so long." I press my lips to his, partly because I can and partly because if I have been asleep since this morning, it has been far too long since I last did.

Cal growls as I grab the back of his neck, pulling him back to the bed with me and deepen the kiss, opening his mouth with my tongue and sucking on his. His growl turns into a moan before he pulls away from my mouth to trail kisses along my jaw and throat. "You make me crazy with that mouth," he groans.

I huff a laugh and press my body further into him, encouraging his exploration to continue south. "You are the one with the filthy mouth, Stud. But I am all for helping you make a mess of it."

Cal reaches down to trail his knuckle through my center, finding me drenched for him. "And it seems that you have no problem making a mess all on your own," he says against my skin, before pulling my nipple into his mouth and biting down.

I gasp at the pain, even as I feel myself dampen further. Lining up his cock to my entrance, Cal thrusts into me in one hard, deep stroke. "Fuck," he groans. "You take me so well."

I pull his mouth back up to mine, kissing him long and slow while he fucks me in a steady rhythm, building up my orgasm from deep within.

"Cal, I'm…"

"Go ahead, Mo Chridhe. Come for me."

Cal continues his efforts long after the last waves of my orgasm wash through me. Once he is sure that I am spent, he fills me with his own release before collapsing on top of me and burying his sweaty forehead into my neck.

"I think we might have missed dinner," I mumble, suddenly remembering that there was an actual reason for this wake-up call.

Cal chuckles. "This is our home—dinner will not be served until we wish it."

Despite being completely entangled, and a little bit crushed by his massive body, I pull away just enough so that I can see his face. "You mean there are people sitting at our table right now, waiting to eat while we bang like horny teenagers down the hall?"

"You started it," he says, not bothering to hide his smirk as I wiggle out from under him.

"Yeah. And now we both finished," I say, wildly gesturing to the cum dripping down my thighs. "Help me clean up so that they don't know why we were late!"

Now he is full-on laughing, huge belly laughs that I let wrap around my heart—even as I frantically move from the bed to the bathroom and then to the wardrobe. "What does someone wear if they do not want a group of bear shifters to know that you are late to dinner because you just got your brains banged out?"

After looking at my options, I realize that I don't have any. The lone outfit that remains is a simple gauzy dress that looks way too much like lingerie to wear to a group event. I can feel Cal step up behind me as I stare at the piece. "Well, that is definitely not screaming innocent virgin," he jokes, wrapping his arm around my waist and grinding his cock against my ass.

"Now is not the time to be hard!" I shout, playfully pushing him away. "I know that you are super busy being gorgeous and trying to stop a war, but do you think you can locate some mice shifters to whip me up a dress to wear to the ball?"

Based on the look of amusement on his face, he at least understood some of my stress ramble. "I have already arranged for a *bear* shifter to take your measurements tomorrow. She came by earlier today while you were sleeping." Moving over to the table near the door, he picks up a package that I hadn't noticed before. "But she did leave this here. The fit might not be perfect, but it will cover more than the scrap of fabric left in the wardrobe." The dress that he pulls out of the package is a beautiful sun dress made up of different shades of yellows, oranges, and golds. "She was going to leave some sleepwear as well, but I told her that you wouldn't need any."

I snort out a laugh before grabbing the dress from his hands and kissing him on the cheek. "Thank you, Cal. This is perfect."

Once I am dressed, I quickly tame my bedhead in the mirror. Cal's arms reach around me, securing a golden necklace with a deep purple gemstone around my neck. My breath catches as the gem settles right over my heart. "This was my mother's. My father had it made for her to match his eyes—though because she was not Sun Kissed, she could only wear it when she was pregnant. She would want you to have it."

"You have your father's eyes?"

Cal nods. "All of the males in our line are born with violet eyes with small flecks of gold. The females, like my sister and Nana, have eyes of pure gold. Most Sun Kissed females are."

"But mine are green."

"They become more golden each day. Look." He turns me back to the mirror—and he is right. My eyes which used to be a vibrant green are now a golden green.

"How is this possible?"

"Magic," he says, as if it is that simple. "Your powers were not awoken until you came to this world. It makes sense that your Sun Kissed traits, like your mark and your eyes, would not reveal themselves until now."

I turn in his arms, tucking my head under his chin. "I love it, Cal. Thank you."

22
The Lady with a Screaming Pussy

Callum

The smile that Willa gives me as we walk hand in hand down the hallway on our way to dinner could feed me for a lifetime. She beams as her golden dress flickers in candlelight, casting a glowing aura around her. I was not planning to give her the necklace until our bonding, but the way that she lit up after receiving it—there is nothing better in this life than that smile.

I truly had not planned to fuck her before dinner either, especially after I took things too far this morning, but it would be dishonest to say that I am not deeply satisfied having my Mate walk into a room full of our clan, smelling so freshly like me.

Approaching the door, I give Willa's hand a reassuring squeeze before entering the dining room—the same one where I had Willa laid out while I gorged myself on her pussy. Walking directly to the head of the table, I pull out Willa's chair for her to take a seat before sitting down on my own. Despite a second chair being provided, I quickly realize that there is only one place setting. The kitchen staff have not provided dinnerware for my Mate. Unable to stop my bear's reaction, a low growl fills the room, silencing the idle chatter occupying the table.

Noticing the reason for my mood shift, Tor begins to stand, ready to retrieve the errant staff. But before he can leave his place, Willa's hand reaches out to hold his arm.

"It's okay," she says quietly. "Cal and I will share. I'm sure that it was just a mistake."

Tor does not look to me for approval. He simply takes Willa's command and nods before he sits back down. We both know that this was more than just a simple mistake—but it is a matter that we can address privately.

"Let's eat," I say before serving Willa and myself the dish directly in front of us—a savory roast.

Just like every time when I eat dinner with my clan, announcing that it is time to eat does not induce anyone to pick up their forks. Some Clan Chief far before my time insisted that he takes the first bite of every meal and therefore it became tradition. A tradition that normally, I would balk at but am thankful for tonight. Lifting my fork, I bring it up towards my lips before diverting the path and feeding it to my Mate instead.

I am not sure if it is the moan that escapes Willa's mouth or the act of feeding her the first bite that has dropped everyone's chins to the floor, but I do love shocking them to silence. Chuckling, I offer her a second bite before finally taking one myself. As soon as the food enters my mouth, the room lets out a collective sigh of relief and begin eating.

Having picked up on the awkwardness followed by the communal ease, Willa brings her hand to her mouth to quiet the snort that bursts from her nose, causing me to laugh, which is then followed by my entire cadre erupting in hysterics while everyone else in the clan are stunned back into silence.

Thus was the cycle for the entirety of the evening meal.

"Are you sure that they are okay with me being here?" Willa asks later, as we clean up before bed. I'm not surprised that she is asking. Dinner was definitely a strange experience.

"Bears are stubborn creatures. As a species, we struggle with change and easily get set in our ways," I start to explain.

"But you aren't like that. And Tor, Colt, Bo, and Adan never treated me like an outsider. Even in the beginning."

"We are all young, Mo Chridhe. Most bears in this clan are several centuries our senior. It will take time for them to adjust to new customs."

She chews on her lower lip, processing. "And I'm guessing a human dropping out of the sky and becoming their whatever I am isn't something they have ever dealt with before, huh?"

"Their Lady," I tell her, brushing my thumb over her lip to soothe the mark left by her teeth. "As the Heart Mate to their Clan Chief, you are their Lady."

"Oh," she says with a small smirk. "And when will that become official?"

"Ceremony or not, you are my Heart Mate. That happened the minute you awoke in this world. But the next bonding sun is in a week."

Finishing up in the bathroom, Willa takes my hand and pulls me over to the bed, turning around so that I can help her undo the clasp of her dress. "What does bonding entail? Ramsey told me a little bit about the bonding process with the wolves and honestly, I have been a little afraid to ask. She said that it was kind of like a wedding and then it jumpstarts a heat. Growing up, we had a cat that would go into heat, and she would scream-meow at all hours of the night trying to attract a horny tomcat to help her out. I don't want to be so needy that my pussy screams until some rando comes and jumps my bones."

"Breathe, love," I chuckle as I press a kiss to her shoulder. "Let's crawl into bed and I will explain everything."

"Do bears even have heats? Is that a part of the bonding?" She asks again as she crawls under the blankets on the bed. I slide in next to her, pulling her body flush with mine.

"Yes, bears have heats. And, yes, the bonding might start a heat for you. As far as I am aware, this has never happened before—between a human and a bear. But I would guess that the magic would react similarly for us as it did between the Nights and their human Mates. However, it would not be 'some rando' who answers your pussy's call. I would be with you every step of the way. Your scent drives me wild every moment of a regular day—but when you are in heat, it is unlikely that either of us will be able to come up for air until it recedes."

"And you would be okay with doing that? I wouldn't want to be a burden." Her voice is so quiet, I'm not sure that she even realized she said the words out loud. Moving her so that she is straddling my waist, I lift my hands to her face and force her eyes to meet mine.

"You are never a burden," I say firmly. "There is not a question I will not answer. There is not a need I will not sate. My food, my gold, my name—the very heart that beats in my chest is *yours*. I do not know who made you believe that you were ever a burden, but I will happily spend the rest of my days proving the falsity of that claim."

I watch as a single tear trails down her face before she quickly swipes it away and brings her lips to mine. When she pulls away, she rests her forehead on mine, breathing in the air that I would willingly give up for her.

"I assure you that spending a heat with you is no hardship for me. In fact, I am quite looking forward to it." Willa softly giggles in response, nestling her face into my neck as I wrap my arms around her in a tight embrace.

"When my grandmother died, I discovered that she was in debt. A lot of debt," Willa explains. "I didn't know it at the time, but she had taken out loans to pay for my activities and schooling. She never made me feel like a burden growing up—but when I found all of those unpaid bills and realized what they were for…" She shakes her head. "I didn't realize that I relied on others as much as I do, despite actively trying not to."

"I understand that—that feeling. Before my family was killed, I did not take my responsibility seriously. I thought that I could do whatever I wanted and that I did not need anything from anyone else. After they were gone, I had no choice but to rely on others despite not knowing who I could trust. Tor and my friends held me together when the world around me fractured. They helped build me up so that I could become the leader that I needed to be."

"They really care about you," she says quietly, snuggling us further down on the bed so that her head is resting on my chest. "I could tell that day in the meadow. They didn't hesitate to fight with you, to fight for *me* just because of who I am to you."

"I care about them too," I admit. "But I would give them up in a heartbeat if it meant keeping you."

"I would never ask you to choose," she says, yawning as she falls under sleep's spell.

"I know." I kiss her head. "But I would anyway. Every day, in every lifetime—I would choose you."

23
Did We Just Become Best Friends?

Willa

Walking through the halls of the keep, I can't help the blush that warms my face. Cal left earlier this morning to meet with some of his clan members to discuss the encroaching threat of the rebels. I offered to go with him, just in case they needed me to use my magic that I don't actually know how to use, but he promised that they would not be getting close enough to make contact. He just wanted to see it all for himself—but not before making me come so hard that I forgot my own name. The things that man can do with his tongue...

I shake my head, trying to focus on my task for the day—learning my way around the keep. Based on the delicious smell in the air, I must be getting close to the kitchen. Hearing voices, I slow my steps. I don't mean to snoop, but I also feel awkward just walking into a room with people that I don't know, especially if they are in the middle of an argument. Which they clearly are.

Not sure how to proceed, I look over my shoulder at my shadow—who has been doing a remarkable job of blending in. Moments later, Colt joins me at my side. "Do you think everything is okay?" I whisper so quietly, he probably wouldn't be able to hear me if he was a human.

"There is only one way to find out," he replies with a smirk before leading the way through the large double doors.

As soon as we enter, the voices stop.

"Father," Colt says in greeting, not making any attempt at greeting the other bear in the room. Arturas does not spare his son more than a quick glance before returning his focus to the woman standing before him. Aurora. My biggest fan.

"Hello," I say, somewhat annoyed that neither of them acknowledged my presence.

Still standing in a heated silence, Colt crosses the kitchen to where some breads, fruits, and cheeses are laid out. "Are you hungry?" he asks me.

Following his lead, I square my shoulders as I brush past the squabbling lovebirds and pick up what appears to be some kind of grape, popping it into my mouth and carrying on as if this isn't one of the most awkward moments of my life. Colt and I work together to fill our plates before leaving to exit the kitchen to find a place that is more comfortable.

"Give a message to the Chief for me, will you?" Aurora's voice cuts through the room. I'm not sure if she is talking to me or to Colt, but I turn to face her.

"What message would that be?" I ask.

"The tailor arrived earlier this morning, but I sent her away," she explains with a sneering smile on her face. I can feel Colt tense, emitting a soft growl behind me.

Doing my best to keep my own irritation in check, I take another bite of fruit before replying. "Why would you do that?"

"I know that he is not to be disturbed in his chamber. That is why I have been demoted, is it not?"

"You were moved to your current position because you overstepped—clearly you have not learned your lesson since you have done it once again. The tailor had an appointment with me, not my Mate. It is unacceptable that I was not notified of her arrival. But don't worry, I will make sure that Cal hears your message loud and clear. I'm sure it will not be long until you hear his response."

Colt follows me out of the room, first holding the door open for us both and then offering me a high five as we make our way back down the hall. "You are so badass," he tells me with a smile. I snort, feeling more irritated than proud, but unable to stop the laugh at hearing a bear shifter use a term like "badass."

"Is there any way that we can get the tailor back here? Or we can go to her? I feel bad that she was sent away due to Aurora's pettiness."

"I can take you to her," he offers. "Mira does not live in the keep, but her home is not far. Only about a 5-minute walk from the gate."

"Why doesn't she live in the keep?" I can't imagine Cal not offering her a room like he has done for everyone else in the clan.

"She will come and stay at the keep if danger approaches but prefers to keep her family home as her permanent residence. She shared the home with her grandparents until they passed, and now I think it brings her some peace—staying and working in the same space that her family created." I don't miss the smile that spreads across his face as he talks about her.

"Are you…"

"No," he shakes his head. "At one time we thought we might be—but the heart string never formed. Delays can happen, but it is unlikely at this point."

"I'm sorry," I tell him. And I really mean it. It is clear that he cares about her deeply. "Being Heart Mates isn't required for being in a relationship, though, right?"

"Not for most. But it is for me." His voice is so quiet. So *sad* that I can feel my own heart break a little for him.

That is when I see it. I didn't notice before because they are muted, but Colt's eyes are a purplish blue with flecks of gold glinting in the sunlight. "You are Sun Kissed?"

"My mother was. My parents were not Heart Mates. She found herself pregnant after a heat cycle, despite taking preventative teas, and decided to stay with my father. The powers should not have passed to me. It is unheard of for non-Heart Mates to produce a blessed cub. If I wasn't...Mira and I could..." He takes a deep breath, clearing that line of thought away. "If I have any chance of continuing on the Sun Kissed line, I will need to find my Heart Mate."

Our conversation moves on to lighter topics as we finish our snack and make our way out of the keep. But I can't help but think about Colt's situation. What would Cal have done if one of his previous lovers became pregnant? Would he have formed a mate bond with them? Would he have left them behind once I fell from the sky? My face burns in anger as I realize that is the exact situation Aurora was trying to orchestrate—to force Cal into accepting a relationship that he did not want. And for what? What was her motive? Because it certainly was not done with good intentions as Cal once believed. If that were the case, she would have stopped the first time that Cal refused one of her "gifts." She would have stopped long before Cal was run out of his own house to avoid whoever she was going to force on him next.

Approaching an adorable cottage straight out of the pages of a storybook, I am forced to put those thoughts on the back burner and take in the beautiful woman in front of me. She is tall, much like the other shifters that I have met, but she is somehow still petite. Her features are almost pixi-like, and her movements are fluid, graceful. Who knew I could be so mesmerized by someone walking? I think I have a girl crush.

"You must be Willa," she greets, pulling me into a hug and causing Colt to chuckle at my side.

"I'm so sorry that you were sent away earlier," I apologize.

Mira scoffs, "Don't worry about it. I know that it was just Aurora being Aurora. She isn't taking her new role very well, is she?"

"You've heard about that, huh?"

"Oh, honey, I think everyone has heard about how you and Cal put her in her place." Mira's voice is warm as she laughs and pulls Colt into a hug as well. Seeing how they both hold on to each other a little tighter than necessary, I look away, offering them as much privacy as I can.

"So, you are probably here for some clothes," she says, leading the way into her home. Colt stops outside the door, not entering behind me.

"She is going to want to measure and dress you. I will just wait out here."

"Thank you, Colt. We shouldn't be too long," I tell him.

He laughs. Loud. "It is cute that you think that."

I continue into the house, not completely sure where she wants me, but unable to stop myself from snooping around. I can understand why Mira chooses to remain here, instead of moving to the keep. Every square inch of this place is layered with love. A worn blanket draped over a reading chair. Books scattered throughout the space, open to whichever page she left off on. Artwork and swaths of fabric adding splashes of color to the stone walls. The keep is beautiful too—don't get me wrong—but *this* is a home. Mira walks back into the room carrying a bundle of fabrics and a teapot, which is precariously balancing at the top of the pile.

"Thanks," she says, as I make a grab for the tea. "I am a firm believer in only making one trip if I can at all manage it." Mira motions towards the coffee table. When I bring the teapot over, she shakes her head and giggles. "I meant for you to climb up there, but I guess it makes sense for the tea to be placed there as well."

I laugh then too before climbing up onto the table. Tea immediately forgotten, Mira gets right to work, taking my measurements and lifting different fabrics up to see how they look against my skin tone and hair color.

"Have you always been a part of Cal's clan?" I ask, wanting to learn more about everyone here.

"Yes and no," she replies. "My father and his parents and their parents have always been closely tied to the Claws, residing in their clan for as far back as anyone can remember. But my mother is a panther shifter. She was traveling when they caught each other's scents—their hearts brought them together."

"Heart Mates?"

She nods. "When I was a child, the unrest in the bear territories was beginning to rise, so my parents moved back to my mother's land. They tried to convince my grandparents, my father's parents, to move with them but they did not want to leave their home—this home. After my parents died, I moved back here to be with my grandparents, and this is where I have remained."

"You didn't want to stay with the panthers?"

Mira shakes her head. "I never really fit in there. Panthers are very secretive and they are not as welcoming as other species. I have never been able to shift. So, they did not know what to do with me. I can feel my animal. She is just suppressed." Mira shrugs. "Here, I am different too. But I am not treated as if I am."

"I'm glad that you have found a place here," I tell her.

"Me too," she says quietly, looking over at the door before turning back to her work.

Just like Colt predicted, I stay at Mira's until almost dinner time. "Will you be coming to the keep for dinner tonight?" I ask on my way towards the door.

"I'm not sure if I should," she says, biting her lip.

"You are always welcome," I tell her. "It would be nice to have someone there who I actually enjoy talking to. Well, other than Cal and his band of merry gentlemen."

"What did you call me?" Colt shouts from the other side of the door.

"Maybe gentlemen isn't the right word. Miscreants? Scoundrels?"

"I didn't think that you liked me being a gentleman," Cal's voice calls out from where Colt is stationed.

My heart flutters at the sound of his voice. I take the last couple of steps before flinging the door open and jumping into Cal's waiting arms. "Miss me, Mo Chridhe?" he asks against my neck.

"Maybe a little," I reply coyly, inhaling his scent.

"Is that all?" he chuckles.

"Well, I have been thoroughly distracted making a new friend," I tell him, nodding my head towards Mira as she exchanges quiet words with Colt.

"I'm glad," he tells me, kissing me soundly on the lips.

"Did you just get back?" I ask, ignoring the fluttering that is now happening much lower than my heart.

"Yes. We were just passing back through and I saw Colt waiting outside the cottage. I didn't realize that you would be meeting with her here."

"About that…" I go on to tell Cal about our run in with Colt's father and Aurora in the kitchen. "But it all worked out because Colt brought me here. And I'm glad that he did. It gave Mira and I a chance to hang out. I just wish your aunt didn't hate me so much. She wouldn't even return my 'hello' when we walked into the kitchen."

I see Cal look over to Colt, where the latter shook his head before turning his attention back to his conversation with Mira.

"I will talk to her," he tells me. I'm not sure what good that will do, but I nod my head anyway. Whatever is going on with Aurora and Cal runs much deeper than her small displays of disrespect shown towards me.

Cal takes the bag of clothing that Mira put together for me before guiding me back towards the keep.

"Willa held her own against Aurora," Colt says as he runs to catch up. When I see that he is alone, I can't help but feel a little disappointment. I was hoping that Mira would be joining us.

He must notice, so he explains, "Mira really only comes for dinner at the keep if it is a special occasion. She prefers her own space."

"I hope I didn't make her feel uncomfortable by inviting her."

He smiles. "You didn't. She will appreciate the gesture more than you know."

Turning towards Cal, Colt asks for an update on the rebels. They talk for the few minutes that it takes to get back to the keep before we split off to head towards our quarters.

"So, the rebels are moving closer, just like we were told?" I ask once we are back in our rooms. Cal places my new clothes into the wardrobe before turning and pulling me into his arms.

"Yes," he says, kissing my neck. "But I don't want to think about the rebels right now. It has been far too long without your body wrapped around mine."

"You made me come this morning before you left," I remind him, holding back a moan as his lips brush against my pulse point.

"Every moment spent apart is one moment too long. I *need* you, my love. I need you wet." He nibbles on my jaw. "I need you moaning." He pulls my dress over my head. "I need you on your knees." Without a single thought, I drop down, kneeling before him, wet and wanting.

24
Dinner and a Show

Callum

"Do you want to please me, Mo Chridhe?" I ask, keeping my words slow as I unfasten my pants. "Will you be my good girl tonight?"

Willa nods enthusiastically, letting out a small moan as my cock springs free.

"We only have a little while before we will be expected at dinner. Will you follow my directions?"

"Yes," she pants, not taking her eyes from my cock.

"I am going to fuck your mouth, my love. Are you okay with that? Will you take my cock down your pretty throat?"

Willa's tongue darts out to wet her lips as she nods.

"And you won't come until I tell you to. Do you understand?"

"Yes, sir," she replies, a growl of pleasure escaping my chest at her words of submission.

"Fuck," I groan, pressing my cock into her waiting mouth. "Tap my legs if it is too much, sweetheart." That is all the warning I give her before I thrust in further, hitting the back of her throat and holding myself there. I can feel the moment that her throat relaxes, allowing even more of my length to enter her. "Look at you, taking my big cock into your body like you were born to please me." Wiping the tears from her cheeks, I hold eye contact with her until she gives me a little nod. Then I fuck her hard. Taking only enough care to know that my piercings are not going to chip her teeth, I thrust in and out of her mouth, savoring the feel of her wet mouth taking me so well. My bear grumbles, reminding me that she is going to be bruised after this, but I can't make myself stop when she reaches up to grab my balls, working one of her fingers back towards my ass. Applying the lightest amount of pressure makes me erupt, filling her mouth so full of my seed that it drips out at the corners of her mouth.

I can see as she struggles. Not with swallowing it all down, but with resisting touching herself. Reaching my hand down, I gently pull her to her feet before crashing my mouth down onto hers, tasting myself on her lips. Willa presses her body into mine, seeking a release but not finding it for herself.

"You did so well, my love," I praise. "You will be rewarded for that later."

Kissing her one more time, I turn and head over to the wardrobe, selecting a clean pair of pants for myself and a pretty dress for my Mate. "Our game is going to continue through dinner, but I do not want you to be submissive in front of everyone else," I explain. "Can you do that?"

Willa clears her throat before answering, "Of course."

As she gets dressed and fixes her hair, I make a small request with Adan who was waiting for us just down the hall, before Willa and I find our way to the dining room.

At the head of the table, sit two place settings but only one chair. It appears someone is still playing petty games. Too bad for them, I don't mind being my Mate's seat, whether it is my knee, my cock, or my face, she will always have a place with me.

Everyone in my cadre stands to offer their chairs, but I have them sit back down before pulling Willa down onto my lap. Covered by the table and her dress, I snake my hand towards her cunt, spearing two fingers into her wet heat, and keeping them there as I address the table. Willa bites her lip to hide her surprise but doesn't make any indication that she is uncomfortable with this part of our game. Perfect.

"Instead of eating family style tonight, I thought we could try something new. Adan..." Adan stands and walks towards the door that leads to the kitchen, ushering our wait staff in for the night. "Aurora will be serving us all tonight. Starting with my Mate."

Other than the loud scoff coming from Arturas and the stifled chuckles coming from Tor and Colt, the rest of the room takes in this change in events as they would anything else I propose—silent approval. Bears might have strong opinions, but any decision made by the Clan Chief is rarely met with resistance.

Signaling once more with my hand, we all wait in silence as Aurora steps forward to serve us dinner. When she attempts to place the first cut of meat on my plate, I grab her wrist.

"It is improper to serve anyone other than the Chief first," she scolds quietly.

"You will serve my Mate first despite whatever archaic notions of propriety you insist on," I reply. "Willa will always be served before me, even if it is the last morsel in the land. Do I make myself clear?"

"Yes, my Chief," Aurora says through gritted teeth as she tries to withstand the dominance that I wove within my words.

"Fucking bastard," Arturas mumbles under his breath, as if that would stop any of us from hearing it.

"I didn't quite catch that. Do you have something to add, Arturas?" Willa asks, pulling a hum of approval from my chest.

He stares down at his plate, feeling chastised—but it isn't enough. The minutes tick by as he remains silent. "Did you catch what he said, Stud?" she asks as she turns slightly to face me. "Because to me, it sounded like he wanted to sort out that latrine situation that we passed on our way back into the keep today."

I snort a laugh before schooling my features back into mock seriousness. "Yes, my love. I do believe that is what he said." Turning back to face Arturas, I continue, "It is so kind of you to volunteer for that job. Best get to bed early tonight. You are excused."

Once we are all served, I send Aurora away as well, adding a lightness back into the room that had been stifled from their bad attitudes. We all fall into easy conversation as we enjoy our dinner. Tor and I update the clan on what we found during our reconnaissance mission today—basically that we need to prepare for an attack at our wall within the next month. Additionally, I deliver the news that Willa and I will be bonding at the upcoming bonding sun—something that everyone was expecting and genuinely seems excited about.

The entire meal, I pepper Willa's body with kisses, slowly fucking her with my fingers under the table, keeping her ready and needy for the reward that she has earned. "You are being such a good girl for me," I whisper low in her ear, ensuring that my voice is quiet enough that nobody else will hear. My words cause a flutter in her heart—in our hearts—as she squirms against my cock. The motion pulls a groan from me that certainly didn't go unnoticed. Tor raises his brow while Colt, Adan, and Bo openly snicker in response.

"Time for bed," I growl, standing abruptly and picking up Willa in one fluid motion.

"But we haven't had dessert yet," she protests.

"I will have some delivered to our room." I nip at her ear, causing bumps to raise all over her pale arms. "I have an appetite for something else at the moment."

Willa squeals as I lift her over my shoulder, taking off in a sprint back to our quarters. Once inside, I slam the door shut with my foot, not stopping until Willa is within throwing distance of the bed. Her laughter fills the room as I do just that, crawling over top of her. "How attached are you to these clothes?" I ask, slightly out of breath.

"Don't you dare," she says, working her hand between us so that she can undo the fastenings enough to slide the garment off her body. "You can't just rip all of my outfits off of me."

"You denying me the pleasure makes me want to do it even more," I tell her between kisses, though I do help her gently rid her of any and all barriers as I work my way down her body. "Beautiful," I tell her as I take in the sight of her pussy, glistening with arousal. I swipe my tongue through her center, her sweet flavor bursting on my tastebuds. "Are you close, my love?"

She moans in response. Her desire from being played with at dinner soaks her thighs. "Tonight, you do not need to ask before you come. I am going to try some new things with you. Is that okay, Mo Chridhe?"

"Yes, sir," she replies. "I want to try everything with you."

"Good girl." I reward her by sucking her clit into my mouth. Reaching around and finding her discarded clothes, I wrap the fabric around her wrists, positioning them above her head. "Does that feel comfortable? Not too tight?" I trail my hand down her arm, over her breast, and snake it behind, squeezing her ass and pulling her pussy closer to my waiting mouth.

"It feels so good."

Giving her clit several more flicks with my tongue, I pull back and bring my hand down firmly on her delicate skin. The sting pushes her over the edge as she convulses and comes. "That's one," I say as I bring my mouth back down to soothe her blushing core.

"Fuck, Cal," she moans as ripples of pleasure run through her.

Trailing my fingers through her release, I drag them up her body, swirling them around her nipples before painting her lips. Willa's tongue darts out right before I press my mouth to hers, swallowing her moans and allowing her to suck her sweetness from my tongue.

Carefully flipping her onto her stomach, I place a pillow under her abdomen for support as I pull her ass into the air and dive back in, groaning at her orange blossom and honey taste. I didn't know that someone could be so delicious. I continue working her with my tongue until her legs shake.

"Cal can I…"

"Come, Mo Chridhe. Push yourself back and come all over my face. Use me. Take the pleasure that you deserve."

Her pussy erupts, spilling down her thighs and onto the bed below us. "That's two," I purr. Cleaning her up with my tongue, I swirl it around her back hole before gently pressing inside. A guttural groan leaves Willa's chest as she pushes back against me again. Taking that as a sign that she is okay to continue, I continue eating her ass, pressing my fingers back inside her cunt.

"I can't," she protests with tears in her eyes. "It's too much."

"Yes you can, sweetheart. You can come again. Do you want me to stop?" I ask, not wanting to push her too far.

"Fuck no," she says sharply. "Don't ever stop."

I chuckle against her as I press kisses all over her skin. "Are you ready for my cock?"

"In my ass?"

I laugh again. "No, my love. In your dripping pussy." I position the head of my cock against her entrance. "I will take your ass, but not tonight. You aren't ready for me there yet." That doesn't stop me from pressing my thumb into her, though. She is so hot and wet, it takes a great amount of concentration to fuck her in slow strokes, drawing out her pleasure and delaying my release for as long as possible until we both detonate with orgasms so strong, I think I might have lost consciousness for a moment.

Collapsing onto the bed, I unbind her hands and drag her body against mine. "Are you okay?"

"Mmhmmm," she mumbles, "but I think I'm dreaming again."

"This is real," I reassure her, kissing her forehead and holding her tightly to my chest as our rapid hearts beat in time with each other.

25
Bared & Bound

Willa

"Mira, you can't just…"

Colt's voice jars me from sleep moments before our bedroom door bursts open. Mira glides inside, not at all concerned with seeing Cal's naked ass or the fact that he is sprawled out on top of me growling in annoyance.

"Good morning, sleepy heads," she sing-songs as she pulls our curtains open, letting in a glow of morning light.

"Is there a reason why you are here, Mira?" Cal asks.

"Well, since Colt has decided that I can no longer stay at my own residence for the foreseeable future, I figured I should get to work on creating Willa's ceremonial dress. Is this not a good time?"

I giggle, knowing without any doubt that this is the punishment that she has deemed appropriate for making her temporarily move into the keep. While I have enjoyed having my new friend so close for the last couple of days, she is a little salty about having her freedom restricted—even if it is for her safety.

"For the thousandth time, it was a suggestion, not a command," Cal grumbles.

"Colt told me that my options were to move into the keep or allow him to move into my small cottage. You know that I cannot have him all up in my business like that," she replies.

"And why is that?" I ask, purposefully stirring shit up.

Cal chuckles against my neck. He told me last night that Mira and Colt have always bickered back and forth, even as kids. When Mira moved away with her parents, Colt was heartbroken. Everyone assumed it was because they were destined. But when she returned, the bond never formed. They returned to their constant back and forth, burying any hopes of becoming more.

"You *know* why," she says between her teeth.

"I don't *know* anything," I fib. "I have guessed a few things. But honestly, I don't get it. I am a recent convert to the forced proximity trope. 10 out of 10 would recommend."

"Clearly I have come at a bad time since you are obviously in need of an appointment with the healer to check your head."

"Yes, this is definitely a bad time. Please go away so that I can get *my* head the attention it needs," Cal tells her, his body still on glorious display as he buries his face further into my hair.

Mira clucks her tongue but makes no move to leave us alone. I reluctantly detangle myself from Cal, wrapping a blanket around my body and tossing another over Cal's ass on my way to the bathroom.

"Where are you going, Mo Chridhe?" Cal whines into the pillow. "I bet she would leave if we just started fucking."

Colt's answering growl from out in the hall tells me exactly what he thinks about that suggestion.

"I promise that I will attend to your head later, Stud," I say to Cal as I come back into the room, placing a quick kiss on his lips. "I really do need to have something to wear for our bonding tomorrow. And, now that I'm up, I'm hungry."

Cal groans but gets up and moves himself into the bathroom, coming back out a few moments later dressed and looking far too good for the small effort he put in to ready himself for the day. "I will bring you some breakfast," he says against my lips before walking towards the door. "Mira, did you eat or would you like me to serve you as well?"

"Well, if you are already going to be bringing some back..."

Cal laughs under his breath. "You are lucky my Mate likes you."

Several hours later, I am exhausted from having Mira hold up, wrap, and pin various fabrics across my body. I thought that she was planning to actually make the dress right now, but all that has resulted from the entire morning are beautifully beaded scraps of fabric that were unlikely to cover an entire boob, let alone all of my parts.

"Done!" Mira exclaims, only adding to my confusion.

"Um...done with what?" I ask. Done with the beads? Done with that portion of the dress? Done until after lunch? Does 'done' mean something different here?

She looks up at me, tilting her head to the side, clearly confused by my confusion.

"I'm done. Isn't it pretty? I rarely get to work with gold," she gushes over the fabric as it shimmers in the sunshine. It really is beautiful. I'm just not sure what it is.

"Go on, then. Put it on!" she tosses the fabric at me and shoos me into the bathroom.

Still too confused to do anything other than following her direction, I strip off my clothes and stand in front of the mirror, holding the garment up to my body. "Um, Mira? Can you maybe come in and help me?" I ask, having no idea how this is supposed to go on any part of my body.

Opening the door, she laughs, realizing that I have no idea what I am doing. She deftly swipes the material from my hands and proceeds to wrap it around my body, fastening it with hidden loops and ties so that it is covering my nipples and vagina. And by covering, I mean that if the band around my breasts was any thinner, my areolas would be on display, and one wrong move could mean flashing my pussy to the paparazzi Brittney style. Other than the thin band covering my chest, my back is completely bare and there has been essentially no fabric allotted to cover my ass. This can't seriously be what I am supposed to wear during the ceremony, right? I have lingerie that covers more.

"Is there another piece to add to it?" I ask as delicately as I can muster.

"Cal will have some gold jewelry for you to wear," she responds.

All the jewelry in the world is not going to make up for the fact that I am essentially naked. Cal must sense my panic through our heartrate, because only a few minutes pass before he is rushing into the bathroom, finding me mid-meltdown.

He immediately pulls me into his arms, kissing my forehead, and rubbing gentle circles on my back. "What is wrong, my love?"

Noticing for the first time that Mira is no longer in the room, I let it all spill out of me. "All day, we have been working on what I thought would be my dress for our bonding tomorrow and then Mira declared that it was done and I wasn't sure how that was possible since all she was holding in her hands was a beautiful, tiny scrap of beaded cloth. And then she wanted me to put it on but I didn't know how so I asked her to help me and this is what it looks like and how can I possibly get married, or bonded, whatever you want to call it...how can I do that wearing essentially nothing? I asked her if there was anything else to add to it and she said that you would have jewelry for me to wear too but unless you have a full suit of armor, I'm not sure it is going to cut it."

"Breathe, sweetheart," he replies, pressing my face firmly to his chest. I let the steady beat of his heart ground me. "I should have talked to you about our ceremonial wear before letting Mira get her hands on you. I know it might be hard to believe, but I sometimes forget that this world is completely different from the one you know."

An embarrassingly snotty snort escapes me as I laugh despite my tears. "I'm sorry," I say.

Cal spins me so that I am once again facing the mirror, his tall, broad body framing mine. "You have nothing to apologize for. If you don't like the garment, we can choose something else. You can wear anything that you like."

Looking closer at how the fabric catches the sunlight, I can't help but admit that it is beautiful. If my hair is up or pulled off to my shoulder, my sunburst mark would be the star of the show. Maybe nobody would even notice that my ass is out.

It is just very different from the style of wedding dress that I always thought I would have.

"Is this what is traditionally worn for bonding?"

"Yes. For Sun Kissed pairings, this is traditional. When non-Sun Kissed bond, they are able to wear other styles of dress."

"And what will you be wearing?" Would I feel more comfortable if I know that Cal will be just as exposed as me?

"Traditionally, my piercings would all need to be on display, since I do not have a Sun Kissed mark to show."

Turning back to face him, my eyes flick down to his crotch before slowly working their way back up to look at his face. "Oh."

He chuckles. "Yes. Oh." Leaning in, he takes my lips in a gentle kiss.

"I guess I should be happy that my Sun Kissed mark did not show up on my pussy and am allowed even this minuscule amount of modesty."

"I am quite fond of you having your pussy out. I think that maybe Mira should make some slight modifications—maybe eliminate the fabric altogether."

"Naughty," I purr as I bring my lips back up to meet his.

After an almost indecent make-out session, Mira's voice rings out from behind the bathroom door. "Do you guys need another minute or is it safe to enter?"

"Go away," Cal responds as I say, "Come in!" Laughing at the scowl that forms on his face.

Mira walks through the door moments later, not put off at all by the growly grump who is refusing to let me wiggle free from his arms. "I just wanted to check to see if any modifications need to be made now that you have had some time to adjust."

"Yes, actually…" Cal starts but I immediately slap my hand over his mouth, not letting him suggest *less* fabric.

"This is perfect, Mira. Thank you for making this for me."

"Of course! Well, if there isn't anything else, I will see you tomorrow!"

"You aren't coming to dinner?" I ask. I was hoping that since she is staying in the keep, I would have another friendly face at the table.

"Not tonight. Neither will you." Turning her attention to Cal, she asks, "Have you told her anything of importance about the bonding ceremony? Or was it mostly just 'growl, growl…I'm going to bite you and make you really horny, growl…"

"You are going to bite me?" I screech.

"See ya!" Mira shouts as she hightails it out of the room.

Cal takes my hands in his and leads me back into the main room of our suite. "Yes. That is how the bond is sealed. Well, the first part of it. The second act is more private." Cal waggles his eyebrows and dishes out a smirk that would disintegrate my panties if I was wearing any.

I huff out a laugh. "Yes, a lot of sex. I remember you telling me *that* part. But you conveniently left out the biting and the barely there underwear being my only clothing. Is there anything else?"

"The ceremony begins at dawn."

"I have to wake up early?" I whine. "I am *so* not a morning person."

Cal laughs. "I know. Which is why I was trying to let you sleep in this morning, but someone insisted that they needed something to wear tomorrow."

"If I knew that all I was getting to wear was scraps of fabric, I would have made a different decision. This is why you should lead with facts, Stud. I need to know everything that I am working with before I make such a monumentally dumb choice."

"You were very insistent," he teases.

"And you had ulterior motives for keeping me in bed."

"Always," he chuckles.

"So, I have to wake up early to put on less clothes and be bitten by my Heart Mate at sunrise?"

"And we cannot spend this night together."

"What? But why? Is this some antiquated tradition meant to help keep my virginity intact prior to the big day? Because I don't mean to be the bearer of bad news, but that ship sailed a long time ago. And after your little puppet display at dinner the other night, I doubt anyone in the clan believes that you haven't been sampling the goods."

"Even without you being stuffed full of my fingers, they would have smelled me on you."

"Ew."

Cal's booming laugh fills the chamber, making it impossible for me to maintain my pouty disposition. "And, we still have hours before the sun sets," Cal says as he throws me onto our bed and shows me exactly how much he is going to miss me tonight.

"Five more minutes," I grumble, not at all happy about this early start to the day. Despite being thoroughly exhausted by Cal before he left at dusk, it feels like I *just* fell asleep.

Hearing Mira come into the room despite my request, I decide to do the mature thing and pretend like I am still asleep, hugging the blankets tighter to my body and staying faced away from the door. Maybe I can eek out a few more minutes by not rising too quickly.

"Hurry up!" she whispers—only, her voice sounds harsh, gritty. "Bo won't stay knocked out for very long."

Bo? Bo!

Flinging my arms out, I hit the hard chest of a man before a blindfold is forced over my eyes and a hand is clamped down over my mouth, smelling sweet and silencing my cries for help. Everything else happens so quickly, it is almost impossible for me to fight back, though I do flail, kick, and try to make myself dead weight. It is all useless against two bear shifters. I hear a quiet groan from Bo as I am carried into the hall. My abductors notice that he is stirring because they take off at a run, my body jostling over the man's shoulder as my limbs become heavy and I fight the fog that is overtaking my mind.

I need to stay awake.

"We need to take care of this quickly. If he realizes we were involved, even our family ties will not stop him from casting us out." His voice is so low that I can barely hear him over the rumble of his chest.

"He will not find out," she says. "We will do the handover, just like we planned. It will look like the rebels infiltrated the keep and took his precious Sun Kissed."

I can't let them take me from the keep. I need to stay awake. I need to get away. But every moment, my body sinks further under the influence of whatever it was that they made me breathe in.

I can feel my heartrate slowing. Cal will not be able to detect my panic through our shared cadence. He will just think that I am asleep.

Stay awake.

Think.

We are moving quickly through the keep, I don't think that I will have much time before we are clear of the outer wall, where I am assuming the rebels will be waiting.

Think.

Stay awake.

Unlike when I first arrived in this land, I know that this is not a dream. I cannot just make myself wake up. I cannot just dive straight into danger like I did that day in the field.

Using all of the energy that I have left, I wrap myself up with the heart string that connects Cal to me, knowing that it might be the only way I will ever feel a part of him again.

"Please be okay."

26
Blood Betrayed

Callum

I wake, clutching my chest and knowing with absolute certainty that something is wrong.

The ache is so intense, I stagger as I stumble out of the spare bedroom that I claimed for the night with only one destination in mind. I *need* to make sure that Willa is okay.

Seeing Bo holding his head as he winces in pain, I roar, waking everyone in the keep. The door to my suite is open. Willa is gone.

Tor, Colt, and Adan rush into the hall moments later. Adan falls to his knees next to Bo, checking for any wounds other than the obvious blow to his skull.

"What happened?" I ask through gritted teeth.

"I'm sorry," Bo says. "They knocked me out. Hit me with something and then put a cloth over my nose before I could shift."

"Rebels?" Tor asks. But Bo shakes his head.

"Who?" I demand.

"Arturas," he growls. Doing his best to turn his focus to the male next to me, he adds, "Aurora was with him."

Tor, Colt, and I leave Bo and Adan in the hall, racing in the direction that they were most likely to go.

"They will not survive the day," I growl. Colt nods. He has never felt an attachment to his father, especially now that his mother is no longer with us.

"I know," Tor says quietly.

"If you cannot be my second tonight, I understand. It will not change anything between us. But she has gone too far."

"I'm with you," he confirms.

As we exit the outer door, a huge blast shakes the foundation, pushing us back against the wall, dust falling from between the stones as the entire keep absorbs the force of the flare.

Knowing that we will gain ground quicker in our bear forms, all three of us shift, racing towards the center of the blast, ready to tear down anyone who stands in our way.

Bursting through the treeline, we all take in the sight.

Scattered in the field, several bears lay unconscious, Aurora and Arturas included. In the center, Willa lays on her side, also unconscious but seemingly unharmed. If she caused an explosion that forceful, she likely passed out from using her magic.

"Secure the site," I command as I race to Willa's side, gently pulling her into my arms.

"Please wake up," I beg, rubbing my hands on her arms and face.

Lowering my forehead to hers, I breathe in her scent which is laced with something else. Different from her orange blossom and honey—but still sweet. A growl tears out of my chest when I recall what Bo had said in the hall. She was drugged, incapacitated. And for what? Why would Aurora and Arturas do this?

Clan members start arriving at the clearing, drawn out by my distress call and the blast that rocked the keep. Forming a defensive stance around me, protecting us from the rebel bears who are lying unconscious in the field.

Standing, with Willa in my arms, I take in the magnitude of what has occurred. I can count at least 30 rebel bears, most in fur, who have been knocked out by my Mate's magic. Looking around at the rebels, I recognize their leader, a large gray bear who is adorned with stolen gold. To his right, in her human form, lies the woman who I kicked out of my bed when we first arrived at the keep with Willa. An uncontrolled snarl peels my lips back as my bear recognizes them as well. Has Aurora been working with the rebels this entire time?

"Wake them up," I growl at Colt and Tor who have their parents restrained. I also nod to the rebel and the she-bear, having them restrained and brought back with us. There are too many rebels for us to take them all, so the leader and this mystery woman will have to do for now. The clan will restrain as many of the rebels as they can out in the field before they wake up.

Walking back to the keep, Willa lets out a pained groan but remains sleeping. I tuck her closer to my chest and don't stop walking until I reach our quarters. Bo and Adan are still in the hall, though Bo looks much better than he did before.

"I'm so sorry, Cal," he says, but I wave him off. This isn't his fault. None of us suspected that our own family would do such a thing.

"Make sure that he sees the healer," I tell Adan. "And then help Tor and Colt secure our prisoners. We are officially at war."

Gently laying Willa down on our bed, I immediately take stock of the room, noting the items strewn around the room. Even though she was drugged, it is clear that she fought back. I am so fucking proud of her.

She groans again, reaching up to hold her head just as Mira walks into the room with a healer. "How long has she been out?" Mira asks.

"Since the blast," I tell her quietly, torn between needing Willa to wake and also not wanting to disturb her rest. Her body needs to recover after using such powerful magic.

The healer approaches slowly, unsure as to how protective my bear is going to be in this situation. When I give her a nod, she quickly begins looking Willa over, not finding more than some bruising from where she was held too tightly. As I suspected, she was drugged like Bo. And is likely overtaxed from magic use.

Willa's whimpers grow louder as her eyes begin to flutter. "Shhh, it's okay," I soothe. "Just take your time."

"Stud?" she asks softly, her voice pained from the ache in her head.

"Yes, Mo Chridhe?"

"Is this a dream?"

"No, my love. This is real. *We* are real."

"Seriously? Because I think I remember taking out a whole army of bears before I passed out."

I can't help my chuckle. "You did, sweetheart. You blasted them all unconscious."

"Cool." She nods her head, immediately regretting the motion. "Would you be totally upset if I sleep through our bonding? I'm so tired."

I don't know how, but I completely forgot about our bonding until she brought it up. "Mira, when is the next bonding sun?"

"Two weeks," she replies. "I will let everyone know that it has been postponed until then."

"What? No," Willa protests. "I don't want to postpone. I want to bond with you."

"I am yours with or without the bonding, Mo Chridhe. But you need to be healed for the ceremony—and for the heat that will follow."

Even in her worn-out, half-asleep state, her cheeks redden at the mention of the heat. "You don't mind waiting?"

"I would wait a thousand years—more, if that is what is best for you."

"Okay," she whispers, sinking further into sleep. I crawl fully into bed with her, not caring that there are others in our room as I pull her body against mine. "One condition," she says, snuggling into my chest.

"Anything," I tell her, meaning it truly.

"No more nights spent apart. I tried it your way once and it wasn't all that fun."

"I'm never letting you out of arms reach again."

"Perfect."

27
Claws Out

Willa

He looks so peaceful as he sleeps, his face softened and his eyelashes kissing his cheeks as they flutter through his dreams.

It is two days after the attack, and he hasn't left my side once. I know that he has things he needs to be doing—prisoners to question and a war to manage—but he has kept us both sequestered in our room, insisting that I rest and recover.

The only people that I have seen since I woke up that first time are Mira, the healer, and Colt. I know that Tor, Bo, and Adan have been taking shifts guarding us from out in the hall, but they haven't entered our room, and Cal has definitely not let me leave our room.

Needing to pee, I slowly work myself out from underneath Cal's protective hold, trying not to wake him. "Where are you going?" he grunts, reaching out for me.

"I'll be right back," I promise him. "I just need to use the bathroom."

"Let me help you," he says, fully awake.

"Are you going to hold my hand as I pee?"

He nods, making me laugh.

"Fine, you weirdo." I grab his hand and pull him with me into the bathroom. "Why don't you run us a bath? Then we can get dressed and find some food. Maybe go and talk to your prisoners while we are at it."

"It's the middle of the night," he tells me as he starts filling the tub with water and oils.

"I know," I tell him, washing my hands before peeling my shirt up over my head. "But I have been sleeping for two days and I'm fine. I promise I feel totally normal. But I am going to lose my mind if I don't leave this room soon."

He looks me over—his eyes focusing on the bruises that still mar my body but lets me tug at the fastenings on his pants before helping me out and removing them by himself with a smirk on his face.

Stepping into the water first, he helps me climb in after him, settling me between his legs as we recline in the hot water. "These should be healed by now," he says, gently running the pads of his fingertips over the purple handprints on my arms.

"I'm human," I remind him. "Bruises can take weeks to fully fade."

"They will not get away with it," he promises.

"I know," I tell him. "What will happen?"

"Arturas and Aurora will likely be sentenced to death." His voice is dark, detached—despite the very real hurt I know he is feeling from their betrayal. "I should have killed them that night. I was going to. But I need to know how long this has been going on. How long they have been working with the rebels."

"It wasn't just because of me?"

"That female, the one who Aurora put in our room the night we arrived home, she was with the rebels. I don't know how many of the females Aurora presented to me were rebels. I just assumed that they were from other clans—but when I saw her knocked out from your blast, I realized that it is possible that she has been working with the rebels for quite some time."

"Why would she do that?"

"I don't know. She must have had a reason. But no reason will ever be important enough to excuse her behavior. If she is not sentenced to death, she will be banished."

"Tor?" I don't need to say anything else—he knows what I am asking.

"He understands. Whatever our decision is, he will support us. He loves his mother, but she hurt you. She drugged you, and Bo, and that is not something that can be forgiven."

"And Arturas?"

"Those are his handprints marking your skin."

I nod, understanding. Arturas will die. Maybe not today or tomorrow. But his fate is already sealed.

I sit with that for a moment, trying to decide how I feel about it. If I were back in Chicago, I would probably think that they deserved the right to a trial. A chance to plead their case before their punishment was decided. But this world is different.

More brutal.

But it is also simpler.

Harsh actions are met with harsh consequences. Arturas and Aurora were planning to hand me over to the rebels, not caring how I would be treated or if I would survive at all. That is an inexcusable action in the eyes of my Mate, and as their Lady, it should have been inexcusable to them as well. They are traitors. And in this world, that means death.

My only real issue is how it may affect Tor and Colt. Regardless of their feelings towards their parents and this situation, they *are* still their parents.

"I want to be with you while you talk to them," I tell Cal, breaking the silence that we had slipped into.

"Are you sure?"

"Yes. I need to face them. I need them to see that they did not break me."

Cal thinks it over for a moment before he nods. "Of course. You will stand at my side, where you belong. If you want to leave, we will go. No questions asked."

"Okay."

"And after, I will kneel and worship you like the queen you are."

I huff a laugh. "I am never going to say no to you getting on your knees for me, Stud."

Walking into the dungeon at Cal's side, I hold back my laugh of disbelief. It would probably be unprofessional to be giggling as we walk towards our prisoners—but this place has a legit dungeon. How is any of this real life? I was magically transported to a world of shifters where my Heart Mate can turn into a massive bear. I live in a castle. Oh, and that castle has a dungeon.

Cal gives me a funny look, probably mistaking my giddiness about the dungeon with what we are down here to do and thinking that he is stuck with a lunatic, but he doesn't seem put off by it. If anything, his face shows a flash of amusement before schooling his features back into a serious glower.

"Bo!" I shout as we approach the cells where he stands guard. I rush towards him, wrapping him in a hug as he hesitates to reciprocate the action—my protective bear man growling low behind me. Ridiculous bear shifters. "I'm so happy that you are okay," I tell Bo, ignoring Cal.

"I'm so sorry," Bo tells me sincerely, making my eyes misty.

"It wasn't your fault." I hold onto him a little longer before Cal pries Bo from my grasp. Making me roll my eyes in his direction and pulling a laugh from Bo. Much better.

"Anything to report?" Cal asks in a low voice.

"Other than being major pains in my ass, they haven't revealed anything," Bo says. I'm not surprised that Arturas and Aurora are not happy with their current quarters. Aurora had an issue with sleeping in the staff wing. I doubt she finds the dungeon up to her standards of comfort.

Slipping past Bo, I round the corner and come face to face with the woman in question. "Remember me?" I ask, wiggling my fingers in a little wave.

"You must help me! Please?" she pleads. "I don't belong here."

"Oh, don't worry," I tell her. "You won't be in here much longer. We just have some things that need to be sorted."

"Yes, please tell Cal that there has been a mistake."

"Sure thing. Just one question. Why did you do it?"

"What?"

"Why did you do it? Why did you betray Cal? The clan? Your son? Why did you do it?"

"Everything that I did was to protect them."

"Oh sure, that makes perfect sense. You betrayed your family, worked with the enemy, and started a war to protect them. I can't believe I didn't come to that conclusion myself."

"You don't know anything about this world," she sneers. "You don't even belong here."

"See, that is where you are wrong," I tell her. "This world might be different from the one that I am from, but I understand family, loyalty, and love—none of which you honored with your actions. And I *do* belong here. Cal and I are fated. It was in my world where I didn't belong. Cal is my Heart Mate. He is my home. There is no other place where I should be."

Cal comes closer then, snaking his hand around my waist and bringing his lips to mine. I knew that he was listening to our exchange, letting me take the lead.

"How long?" he asks after ending our kiss and standing at my side.

"What do you mean?" Aurora asks, feigning ignorance.

"How long have you been working with them? I know that it wasn't just the other night. How. Long?"

Before she can answer a deep laugh comes from a cell on the other side of the room. Moving over to see who it is, I come face to face with a grizzled looking man. Someone I have never seen before.

"Pretty thing," he says, licking his lips. "You do not match what she described as his type. No wonder my females were unsuccessful at getting into his bed. My males will be disappointed. They were looking forward to meeting you."

I scoff, unable to hide my disgust. Cal's answering growl lets me know that he is just as repulsed. "How long?" Cal asks this man, who I am now assuming is the leader of the rebels.

He laughs. "Since before you came out of hiding."

Cal snarls, turning back towards Aurora's cell. She must see the anger in his eyes because her bear tries to rip out of her skin in an effort to protect her from his ire, but the cell is not large enough to accommodate her bear form and the transition stops mid-shift.

"Shift," he commands, lacing power within the word. Bo, Colt, Adan, and Tor all swarm to our backs, falling in line behind their Chief and lending silent support. It is clear to me that she tries to fight the command, but is unsuccessful, shifting and cowering as she wets herself. Cal takes a blanket from the shelves behind us and tosses it at his aunt.

"Why?" Tor asks his mother. "How could you?"

She raises her eyes, looking directly at her son before shifting her focus to Cal. "We needed peace," she explains, defeated. "We just needed a union."

"How many?" he asks her.

"All of them," she admits quietly.

"And you were what? Hoping that I would fuck any willing female you left in my bed, hoping that I impregnated one?"

"There is a prophecy for this war," Tor says. "To stop the war that you ensured would be waged."

"Those are just stories," she tells Tor.

"How can you think that?"

"When the Sun Kissed were first blessed—when the lines were new and pure—it meant something. But now? There is no strength left in being Sun Kissed. What we need are alliances. Not stories and a joke of a Sun Kissed blessing. She isn't even a bear."

"And yet she has been blessed with more power than any of us," Cal's words are calm, deadly.

"She doesn't even know how to use her power," Arturas speaks up for the first time. I honestly forgot that he was here somewhere.

"Maybe not," I reply with a shrug. "But I was able to use it to knock you on your ass even while drugged with whatever you forced into my system. Imagine what I will be able to do once I learn how to use it properly. Too bad you won't be there to see it."

28
Kneeling & Healing

Callum

"Are you sure you are feeling okay?" I ask as I back Willa up to the door leading to our quarters.

After our visit to the dungeon, Willa and I shared a meal with my cadre. It is the middle of the night, but Cook did not mind preparing a meal for us. She has taken quite a liking to Willa and was happy to see her up and moving around.

"I feel great," she replies, pulling my hips flush to her body as my arms come up to rest beside her head on the door.

"No headache?" I nip at her sensitive skin over her pulse point.

"That's not where my ache is." Willa shakes her head as she tilts her hips up to meet mine.

"Where is your ache, my love?" I lower my lips to her nipple, wetting the fabric that covers her peaked bud. Her moan turns into a whine as I pull away, waiting for her answer.

"I'm pretty sure I remember talk of you getting on your knees," she sasses while gripping my shoulders, trying to push me where she wants me.

"Command me, my queen."

Slipping out from under my arm, she lifts her dress over her head before grabbing my hand and pulling me to the sitting area near our fireplace. "On your knees," she says as she lowers herself to the edge of the chair, lifting her legs over the arms of the chairs, opening herself up completely for me.

"Fucking beautiful," I groan, my mouth watering at the view of her glistening center.

"Make me gush, Stud. If you are a good boy, I will let you fuck me after." She winks, my cock jerks, straining and leaving a wet spot in my trousers.

"Keep talking like that and I am going to come before I even get my dick wet," I tell her with a smirk.

"Then you better hurry up and get to work." Willa trails her fingers down her body, not stopping until they reach her dripping cunt. Before she can insert her own fingers, I slap her hand out of the way with a growl and dive in, licking her from ass to clit.

It isn't long before she is writhing, grinding her pussy against my face, and screaming my name as her first orgasm rushes through her.

Pulling her into my arms, I carry her over to our bed, throwing her down and flipping her onto her stomach as I rid myself of my pants. Kneeling back down behind her, I bring my tongue back to lap at her cum. She freezes, her breathing accelerating. I tentatively lick my tongue out, wanting to give her time to come down just a bit before I wind her back up—but her breath catches as she jerks away from my touch.

Standing, I turn her over to her back, seeing her blank stare before a flash of panic enters her eyes and she reaches out to cling to me. "Where did you go?" I ask, unsure as to what just happened.

"I'm sorry," she cries, her tears dripping on my bare chest. "I don't…"

"It's okay," I say, taking her face in my hands, looking into her eyes that grow more golden by the day.

"I couldn't see," she explains.

"They blindfolded you?"

Willa nods. "I forgot until just now. I'm sorry."

"You didn't do anything wrong," I assure her, holding her tightly to my chest and kissing her forehead. "They will pay for everything that they did to you."

She nods against my chest. I hold her until her tears dry up. She has been so quiet, I think she might have fallen asleep.

"Make me forget," she whispers as I gently lay her on the bed. I lower my mouth to hers, promising her with my lips that I will do everything in my power to keep her safe. Positioning myself so that my body is covering hers, I make sure that she can see everything that I am doing. She can look and know that she is safe. Notching my cock at her entrance, I tip my brow to hers, waiting for permission.

"Please, Cal. Help me replace the bad with the good—with us."

Slowly pushing inside her, I do not stop until I am fully seated, pausing only long enough for her walls to stretch around me in the perfect fit.

Taking her mouth again, I steadily work myself in and out of her, filling her in slow, deep thrusts. She clings to me like I am her lifeline, the bite of her nails adding pain to the pleasure that is stirring low in my belly, nearly pushing me over the edge.

Stoking the embers with every glide of my cock in her wet heat, I lower my mouth to her sensitive breasts, knowing that she enjoys her nipples being licked, sucked, and bitten almost as much as her needy clit begs for attention. With every thrust, I press the stud of the piercing that sits at the base of my cock against that sensitive bud, flaming the fire until we both combust, our orgasms burning through us in a blaze so hot, I think we might actually burn up.

Staying inside of her, I roll us so that she is resting on my chest, our bodies slick with sweat, and her head tucked into my neck.

"Is it just the men who get pierced in the Sun Kissed lines?" Willa asks, her voice languid with sleep as her fingers trail lightly over my chest.

"For the ritual, yes. But anyone can have a piercing. Most non-Sun Kissed don't bother, since they are not allowed to wear gold, though jewelry is made with other materials."

"So, if I wanted a piercing, that is something that would be allowed?"

Holding her chin with my fingers, I tip her head so that she is looking up at me. "Allowed? What gave you the impression that you need permission for anything?"

"Other than orgasms?" she asks with a smile.

I snort. "Yes. Other than orgasms."

She pauses a moment before explaining more seriously. "I guess it is less about wanting permission and more about wanting to fit in. Not wanting to do something that would be offensive. I feel like maybe I didn't have the best introduction to this world—with all of the almost being bear food and then messing up Aurora's plans for finding you a suitable match."

I start to refute her claim, but she places her finger over my mouth, silencing me.

"I know that you would not have chosen another—especially after you found me. But there must be others who feel the same way she does. Ramsey told me about the issues that she and her sisters faced with the wolves when they first arrived in this world. With how traditional bears seem to be, it is unlikely that everyone is totally cool with me being here."

"There may be some who feel that way," I agree. There isn't much point in denying it. She is right. If we weren't facing a larger issue at the moment, it is likely that some of the more traditional members of my clan would raise an issue with our bonding. But their respect for me as their Chief outweighs their need to voice personal concerns. "However, it is not their decision. Our pairing is fated—decided by the Sun Goddess herself at creation. And there is no doubt in my mind that you are exactly the person I am meant to share this life with. There is nothing that you could do that would change my opinion on that."

Willa presses her lips to mine, dragging me into an unhurried kiss that I can feel deep in my chest.

"So, if I wanted to get my nipples pierced, you would be cool with that?"

I groan through a laugh as my cock jerks back to attention, still inside her. "Mo Chridhe, the mental image of that alone is enough for me to need to fuck you again."

"Oh, darn!" She cackles, squeezing her muscles around my length. "Better make it fast and dirty. It is way past my bedtime."

29
Piercing Tradition

Willa

"Wake up sleepyheads!" Mira says as she glides into our room, not at all concerned with the fact that we were definitely already awake and absolutely in the middle of something.

"Leave," Cal grunts from between my thighs.

I try to push him away, having lost the orgasm that was building, but he doubles down, refusing to prematurely end what he started.

Mira busies herself with setting down a tray of food, pretending to look through a stack of letters on Cal's desk, and tapping her foot as if we are the ones disturbing her morning.

"Colt!" Cal shouts from underneath the blanket. Within seconds, Colt bursts into the room, quickly averting his eyes right before I throw a pillow over my face—melting into the bed in both embarrassment and intense pleasure as Cal fucks my ass with his finger and eats me out like it is his last meal.

I barely hear the small scuffle over the wet sounds that Cal is making while devouring my pussy. Then the door slams and I shatter, screaming into the pillow as I shake and convulse, my thighs clamping down hard around Cal's cheeks. He laps at me through my release and then works his way up my body with a cocky smile on his face.

"You know that you can't just barge into their room," Colt's voice pierces through my orgasmic haze from out in the hall.

"What I know," Mira replies, "is that if I am forced to stay in this keep for any longer, I am going to go insane. And if I am going to go insane, then I am going to drive them nutty right along with me. Put. Me. Down!"

"I can't do that if you are just going to walk right back in there to disturb them," Colt says, slightly out of breath from the struggle that Mira is no doubt giving him.

"Should we go out there?" I whisper to Cal, who is far more amused by this entire situation than he has any right to be.

"And get in the middle of their lovers' quarrel? I think not," he says, flipping me onto my stomach and slapping my ass. "Thoughts on anal?"

"Right now?" I ask, my words rushing out an octave higher than normal.

Cal's booming laughter fills the room. "I'll interpret that as a maybe later," he says as he thrusts his cock into my over sensitized pussy.

"What updates do you have for me?" Cal asks his clan as we settle around the large dining table for dinner, later that evening.

"The rebel clan's leader has not given us any new information. Based on our own observations, it appears that the rebels are unsure what to do now that they do not have someone giving them orders, but they are still amassing and moving closer to the keep," Adan reports.

"And the rebel woman did not appear to have any real knowledge of what role she was playing in Aurora's scheme. I believe she is one of the leader's daughters. He told her that she had to give you her body as payment for a land agreement."

"What a douche-canoe," I mumble under my breath—though Bo and Tor snicker in response.

"And Aurora and Arturas?" Cal asks.

"Still locked up, but not talking—to us or each other," Tor responds.

"It's amazing what a little jail time can do to a relationship," Colt adds. "Not so loving when there are chains involved."

"Unless you use them right," I contribute, smirking when I get a pleased growl out of Cal. Mira giggles and gives me a high five. She might be annoyed that we care enough about her safety to make her stay here, but it really is nice having a friend at the keep.

"Have we heard back from Paw or Maw?" Cal directs his question at Tor.

Tor shakes his head.

"Do you think they will come?" I ask. I knew that Cal had sent messages to the other Clan Chiefs, telling them about the prophecy and asking for aid, but he has not shared more.

"I hope so," he responds. "Sol and Caz came back out of hiding shortly after I did, rebuilding their clans the best they could. I am unsure as to whether they even have a force to supply."

"Do they live close?" I realize that I have no idea how large the bear territory is. I certainly have not seen much of it, having been unconscious for most of the journey from the mountain into Nightfury.

"Caz is several days north, on the other side of the mountain pass. Sol is to the west, sharing the rest of the panther border with me and stretching to the sea. Though technically, it is all one territory. We have had to split it so that we can more effectively monitor the rebels."

"Are we sure that this prophecy is real?" One of the older males asks.

"Yes." Cal leaves no room for argument. I mean, *I* think that the prophecy is real—mostly because I was magically transported here from another world and there must be a reason for it other than having the best sex of my life, right? But I can't blame someone for questioning the validity of it.

"Moving on," Cal continues, "our bonding ceremony will take place in two days' time, during the bonding sun. Because of the treachery that occurred before our last attempt, I will not be spending the night away from my Mate."

Several shocked gasps sound throughout the room. "But the tradition…" one brave soul brings up.

"The tradition is outdated, and I assure you, unnecessary." Cal turns to wink at me, causing my cheeks to flame.

"I can vouch for that," Mira states with a smile. "Just this morning…"

I squeal and slap my hand over Mira's mouth, refusing to let her share the details of the state that she found me in earlier today.

"We can all vouch for that," Colt mutters, smirks appearing on the faces of all of Cal's friends. Damn shifter hearing and poorly insulated castle walls.

"While that may be the case," the older male says, "traditions are there for a reason. It is part of the ritual."

"That is actually incorrect," Tor replies. "The ritual is solely an exchange of bites under the bonding sun at dawn. Over time, other traditions were added in—but they are not vital to the joining of Mates."

"The traditions are there to protect the female," the older man argues.

"I do not need protection from Cal," I tell him firmly. "His presence alone would have made it unlikely that Aurora and Arturas would have attacked. Or, if they still thought it was a good idea, he would have killed them on the spot to protect me. I am safest with him."

Cal yanks my chair, pulling a surprised gasp out of my lungs before sealing his mouth to mine and turning it into a moan. He kisses me slow, but unyielding—pressing his tongue into my mouth. Exploring. Loving. Adoring. The cadence of our shared heartbeat picks up and I can *feel* his care for me, as if it was something tangible that I could hold in my hands. I let it wrap around my own heart as I push my love into him as well.

I have never loved another before. Not like this. Not in an all-consuming, need it to breathe, can't imagine how I ever lived without it kind of way. The logical part of me knows that it is probably because of our Mate bond—the heart string that Cal told me about—pulling us together time and time again. But I also think that it is just Cal. In the way that he cares for me. The way he protects me. The way that he overpowers my senses, disorienting me in the most blissful way. My heart stopped and restarted for him. And it will continue to beat to his rhythm for this lifetime and the next.

Remembering that we are not alone, I break the kiss before I climb into his lap and start dry humping him. As if he can read my thoughts, Cal snorts out a laugh and adjusts his cock in his pants.

"So," I say, ready to move this conversation on from the clan's disapproval. "Who here wants to pierce my nipples before the big day?"

An uproar of protests from the older clan members and raucous laughter from Cal's friends fill the room, descending dinner into pure chaos. Apparently, that wasn't the right thing to say to gain the clan's approval.

30
Heart Wide Open

Willa

"Are you sure that you want to do this now? We could wait until after the bonding. It would heal faster."

Cal's concern for me gaining a couple more tiny holes in my body is cute. I can't hold back my giggle.

"I want to do this now," I tell him for the four-hundredth time. "I want it done before our days long sex session. Think about how awesome it is going to feel."

"And despite my attempts at annoying you, I have zero desire to become an active participant in your heat," Mira chimes in from across the room where she is sanitizing her needle. This piercing situation is far more Sandra-Dee sleepover than I pictured, but I am kind of here for it.

"Who did your piercings?" I ask Cal.

"My father," he tells me. "When I had my 15th birthday. Though, I have added a couple more since then."

Letting my curiosity get the best of me, I ask, "Did Colt do the ritual at the same time?"

"Yes," Cal says as Mira fumbles the needle and starts over on the sanitization process, her face turning bright red.

Noticing the same thing, Cal continues, "But he also has added more over the years," making me laugh as Mira becomes even more flustered.

"Does he have my favorite one?" I ask, knowing that Cal will keep this going as payback for all of our early morning wake-up calls that we have endured since Mira moved into the keep.

"Not yet. I will be sure to let him know how much you enjoy it. I know that he would get it to make his future female pleased."

Mira hisses before turning to face us again. "Are you ready? I am suddenly feeling very stabby." She lifts the needle up, the metal glinting in the beams of sun that fill the room.

"Touchy," I snicker under my breath.

"Maybe if Colt would get touchy, this wouldn't be a problem," Cal whispers before nipping at my ear.

Letting my dress slip down, I bare my breasts—ready to be stabbed. Cal stands at my back, reaching his hand up to support my boobs while Mira approaches with the needle and the matching golden earrings that Cal found in his family's vault.

When I asked him how he still had so much gold after his family was murdered by the rebels and the keep was looted, he explained that most of their golden jewelry was kept deep underground in vaults that the rebels did not know to look for. They took whatever they could find from the building, and burned everything else, but the vaults kept most of it safe. When he came back out of hiding, he knew exactly where to look for it—though most do not know the correct passages to take underneath the keep to get to the vaults.

The rings that he offered me are beautiful—small golden hoops with a tiny purple gem on each. They will match my necklace and Cal's eyes.

"Now is probably not the time to tell you that I have never actually done this before, huh?" Mira keeps enough humor in her tone to make me question whether she is serious or not. Cal's answering growl has me believing that she was telling the truth.

"Just take a deep breath, Mo Chridhe. I will hold you steady."

Shutting my eyes, I take a deep breath before feeling the quick, sharp feeling of the needle piercing my skin and then the almost numb burn that follows. I keep my eyes closed, not sure how my body will react to seeing a needle pressing into me. Then, after a little tugging pressure, I feel the slight weight of the ring settle, pulling my nipple ever so slightly and forcing me to bite back a moan. Cal must catch it though because he chuckles in my ear before licking up my neck.

"Please don't start the growly moans until after I'm done. I got more than enough of a show yesterday," Mira says. "Just one more."

The second piercing seems to go even quicker than the first and by the time the ring has been placed, I am very much ready for Mira to leave.

Cal must be in full agreement because he silently dismisses her with a nod towards the door.

"Does my Mate like a little pain with her pleasure," Cal teases as he flicks his tongue over my tender nipples. "These are going to be fun to play with once you are healed."

I cry out as he gently tugs on the golden hoop, my arousal slickening my thighs. "Please Cal," I beg, not totally sure what I need but trusting that Cal does.

Not taking his mouth off of my breast, he backs me up until my calves hit our bed, forcing me to fall backwards onto the mattress. Cal falls with me, landing with his hands next to my ears so that I am not crushed under the weight of him.

"Are you hungry, my love?" he asks as he continues winding me up with his mouth.

"Food?" I ask breathlessly. "How are you thinking about food right now?"

He chuckles. "We need to be in bed early tonight because of the bonding tomorrow. You will need your energy for the heat that follows. Let me feed you before I fuck you."

I know that he is right. From everything that he has told me about the heat, I will need food now before it starts. But I am already aching so bad. "How about I eat while you eat?" I suggest, rubbing my thighs together.

He laughs again. "Whatever my girl needs. Bo!"

Seconds later, Bo and Adan stick their heads in. Cal keeps his body covering mine, not at all weirded out by the fact that if they heard his voice that clearly, they will definitely be hearing more in a little while.

"Can you get us a tray of food? I would go myself but it appears my Mate requires my mouth."

"Oh my god!" I screech over the sound of Cal's laughter.

"It's time to wake, Willa." Cal's voice gently pulls me from sleep. I groan, not wanting to leave the comfort of our bed at this ungodly hour.

"Five more minutes," I plead.

"Mira will be here any minute to help get you ready."

Rolling over onto my stomach, I hiss out a breath—having forgotten about my new jewelry.

"Why can't you just help me get wrapped up in that thin strip of fabric that Mira calls an outfit?"

"We have already broken enough traditions—I think my clan would be far more amiable if we honor at least a couple of them. I am not supposed to see you until dawn breaks."

"So, we are just going to pretend that you didn't screw my brains out last night?"

"Personal honor protector, reporting for duty," Mira says, her voice dripping with humor despite the early hour.

I snort out a laugh.

"I will see you soon," Cal says as he presses a kiss to my forehead.

Once he leaves, Mira crawls into bed with me—her chipper mood immediately deflating into something more appropriate for waking before the sun. "I am going to move back in with the panthers," she says with a yawn. "Their bonding rituals happen in the afternoon."

"Pack me in your suitcase?"

Mira laughs. "I have a feeling your Mate wouldn't be okay with that."

I sigh in agreement. "Plus, I need him for all of the sex. After his pierced cock entered the chat, there was no going back."

"Okay, fine. We should probably get you ready then."

Begrudgingly, I climb out of bed, get myself cleaned up, and let Mira wrap me up like a kinky Christmas present, polish me with oils, add swirls of golden paint to my exposed skin, and style my hair so that it is not covering the Sun Kissed mark on my back.

The end result is far more rave-like than I typically go for, but I can't help but admit that I do look good. The paint catches the firelight, and I know that it will reflect the rising sun in a beautiful shimmer. Even the dress, if we are still calling it that, only helps to emphasize the markings all over my body.

"It's time," she declares. I follow Mira out of the keep. On our way out of my bedroom, we picked up Bo and Adan, who were still on watch guard duty from the night before. Arriving in the clearing—the same one where I was brought by Aurora and Arturas—the night sky slowly recedes to allow the first rays of pinks and yellows to show.

Standing in the center, Cal locks eyes with me and everything else around me fades away. Nothing else matters but this pull in my chest that tells me that I have finally found my place in the world. I am finally home.

"You look beautiful, Mo Chridhe." Cal reaches out for my shaking hand. "From the moment you awoke in this world, something ancient stirred within me. My heart, once steady and solitary like the mountain winds, found a rhythm it had never known—a heartbeat that matched your own. It was as if dawn broke early, and the light found corners of me I thought long lost to shadow. In that instant, I knew you were not just a visitor to this wild world. You are *my* world.

"The bond of Heart Mates is sealed at dawn, when the light is still soft, and the world still listens. So let the morning witness this promise. I am yours, utterly and without end. Flesh, fur, heart, and spirit. Let my strength shelter you. Let my wildness thrill you. And let my passion be the fire that warms you every night. I will love you until the sun forgets to shine."

Cal reaches his hand up, using his thumb to swipe the tears that are soaking my cheeks. I take a moment to breathe before I speak.

"I've always been a 'go big or go home' kind of girl. Straight-A student, valedictorian, hell-bent on collecting gold stars like they meant something. And then I woke up in the middle of a field—grass in my hair, heart pounding in my chest like it was hearing music for the first time—and you were there, all bear-like and broody and beautiful, charging in to save me like some wild fairytale. I thought that it was a dream because real life does not come with handsome shifters who look at you like you're the answer to a question that they've been asking their whole lives.

"But it wasn't a dream. It was you." My voice has started to crack as fresh tears track down my face.

"And somewhere between that first heartbeat in this world and the moment I realized you weren't about to vanish into thin air, my priorities shifted. Suddenly, I didn't need medals, or trophies, or some title to prove I'm enough. All I wanted—all I *need*—is you.

"You, with your enormous heart. You, who looks at me like I matter more than anything. You make me better, not by changing me but by seeing me. All of me. Loud, stubborn, passionate, me. And somehow, you still decided that I'm yours.

"I promise that I'll never stop challenging you—because I know you secretly love it. I promise to walk beside you, sass intact, heart wide open. With you, this wild, magical, impossible life suddenly makes sense. I don't need gold stars anymore—not when I have you. I love you."

Cal's lips crash into mine before I finish my last word. "Are you ready?" he asks against my lips, not wanting to break our kiss.

Nodding, I look into his amethyst eyes, the golden flecks flaring in the light. Moving his lips down to where my shoulder meets my neck, he sinks his teeth into my flesh, licking away the sting before pressing my mouth to his own neck. Taking a deep breath, I bite down until I can taste his blood. The burn from the bite on my neck begins to spread through my body, settling as an almost painful ache in my core.

Cal's nostrils flare at the blooming scent of my arousal. Within seconds, he is lifting me into his arms, running us back into the keep while swallowing my moans as I rub my thighs together, desperate to find relief.

"Cal, it hurts. I need you to touch me," I whimper in his arms.

31
Heat & Eat

Callum

"I know, my love."

Willa's heat hit faster than what is typical after bonding ceremonies. Whether it is because it is her first heat, I am unsure, but as soon as I scented her arousal in the field, I knew that I needed to forego the other formalities of the ceremony to get her inside and filled as soon as possible.

Willa writhes in my arms as the magic of our bonding spreads throughout her system—changing her at her core. Just like with the Nights and their human Mates, I believe Willa will gain some of my magic. She might not ever be able to shift into a bear, but she will have faster healing, an extended lifespan, and will be changed reproductively so that she will be able to carry our cubs. With that will come painful heats that will only be quelled by the joining of our releases.

I can feel sweat bead and trail down her back as her internal temperature rises. The sounds coming out of her mouth are a combination of a moan and a whimper.

"Please Cal."

Kicking the door shut behind me as I carry Willa over the threshold to our chambers, I don't stop until we reach the bed.

"You do not need to ask this time, Mo Chridhe. Anything you want. Anything you need. Take it all from me."

In a move that completely catches me off guard, Willa spins us around, pushing me down onto the bed beneath her, and impales herself on my cock. A scream of wild pleasure erupts from her throat as she convulses and comes, her honey dripping down my length.

"Can't stop," she groans, rubbing herself against my piercings with so much force, I am worried that she might hurt herself.

"Let me help, my love."

I flip us again, settling myself back between her legs as I grind the piercing at the base of my shaft against her clit. Lowering my mouth to her breast, I gently flick and tug at her nipple ring. Her hand reaches out, pressing my head firmly against her chest—keeping me exactly where she wants me.

I fuck Willa in a steady rhythm; both of our bodies now slick with sweat. When my release barrels through me, Willa's walls suck me in, clamping down around me as I fill her as deeply as I can. Dropping my forehead to her shoulder, I take a moment to catch my breath. But it isn't long before she starts writhing below me, searching for more.

She rotates herself onto her stomach, raising her ass into the air. "Again."

"Shh," I hiss as I open the door just wide enough to accept the meal tray that was delivered. "She is finally resting."

Tor smirks. "It looks like you could use some rest yourself."

I grunt in response. I would be lying if I said I wasn't in need of a reprieve. Keeping up with Willa during her first heat has been more of a challenge than I anticipated—though not an unwelcome one. Stopping only for small breaks where I bribe her into drinking some water, we have been going at it for hours. Now that the sun has begun to set, Willa is finally sated enough to have relaxed into sleep.

"Make sure that she eats," he reminds me quietly. "And I brought extra preventative tea. Do you need anything else?"

I shake my head. "Thank you," I tell him as I retreat back into our bedroom with our supplies.

"Cal," Willa's voice calls out to me as she blindly reaches out for me in the bed.

"I'm here, Mo Chridhe," I tell her softly, approaching with our food. "We need to eat."

"Not hungry." Willa shakes her head as eyelids flutter open, her pupils are blown out with desire. "I just need you."

"You can have me again after you eat."

"Food won't help," she whines, pressing her thighs together in search of relief.

"Five bites, love. Then you can swallow me down."

She tries to protest. The haze of her heat overtaking all of her other senses.

"Five bites," I repeat, bringing the fork to her mouth. She looks at it as if it is the enemy, pressing her lips tightly together. I am torn between wanting to spank her for being a brat or laughing at her stubbornness. "I promise you can have me again after you eat."

Willa sighs before allowing me to feed her.

"Good girl," I praise with each bite taken. After she has made a good effort at clearing her plate and drinking some water, I roll her onto her back, licking a path from her neck down to her navel.

"Fill me," she begs.

"Where do you want me, Mo Chridhe?"

"Everywhere," she moans as my mouth makes contact with her swollen clit.

Flipping myself around so that my knees bracket her head, I lower my face back down to her center, swiping my tongue through her dripping pussy.

"Tap my leg if it is too much," I tell her—my only warning before I thrust my cock down, fucking her throat in deep, long strokes. She gags, but grips my ass, forcing me deeper as she swallows my length down, restricting her breath.

"Do you like choking on my cock, sweetheart?"

She mumbles her agreement, the vibration causing my balls to pull up. Fuck. She is going to make me come.

Gently scraping my tooth against her clit, I force her orgasm before I allow myself to fill her throat.

Pulling myself from her mouth, I flip back around to take her mouth with my own and thrusting my still hard cock into her cunt.

"You are going to give me another one, love. Get my dick nice and wet. And then I am going to fill your ass."

She nods, panting as her heat pulls her further under its spell. Flicking her new piercings with my tongue, I tease her until she is squeezing me like a vice, her heated skin blushing further as she chases her release.

"Come," I command, biting down on her hard bud and letting her scream fill the air.

Flipping her onto her stomach, I press the head of my cock against her back entrance. I have been preparing her for this moment and am happy to see that she is finally ready for me to take all of her.

"Hands on the headboard."

32
Outnumbered

Willa

We are awoken to the sound of a fist rattling the door.

After spending four days in a fog of lust and need, I was finally able to fall into a deep sleep—though it was not deep enough to ignore the chaos that we are waking up to.

Cal shoots out of bed, growling at whoever is disturbing us.

"What?" he asks sharply as the door cracks open.

"The rebels are approaching the keep," Colt tells him calmly. "We are under attack."

That gets my attention. I bolt out of bed, not caring that Colt can see my naked body as I rush around the room to find clothes. Quickly using the bathroom and brushing our teeth, Cal and I make our way to the watch tower guarding the keep.

"How many?" Cal asks as we approach Tor, Bo, and Adan—Colt at our heels.

"Too many," Tor replies. "At least triple what we had anticipated."

"I can help," I offer.

Cal turns to me, reaching up to hold my cheek in his palm. "You haven't recovered enough from the heat, Mo Chridhe."

He is right. I know that he is. But unfortunately for both of us—it doesn't matter. I turn my body east, towards the rising sun. A cold wind bites at my cheeks, but I don't turn away. I welcome the sting as it cools my heated skin. Just past the clearing, a sea of movement creeps through the trees. Tor was right—there are too many of them.

My eyes shift, bringing Cal into view again.

My Mate.

My heart.

Mo Chridhe. Now that his magic is shared with me, I understand the name he had given me at our first meeting.

His large frame stands motionless at my side, seeing the force that we are up against as they approach the clearing.

Our clearing.

Where we stood only a few mornings before, joining ourselves together for eternity. His untamed hair whips in the wind, rattling with the golden beads that are locked onto his strands. Even exhausted, he looks like a king carved from stone—solid, immovable. But I can feel the tremble in his chest—the way that his heart stutters. Not from fear but rage. Worry. For me. For his people.

Our people.

I step closer, resting my hand on his bare arm, and let his body ground me. After days tangled together, with the ache of magic still pulsing in my veins, I feel steadier when I touch him. Like I belong. Like the universe agrees.

"They're coming faster than we thought," he mutters, his voice like gravel dragged through fire.

I nod, swallowing the lump in my throat. "We won't have much time."

Cal's jaw clenches. "You should go inside."

Stepping in front of him, I look up into his violet eyes. "You are not doing this without me."

His eyes search mine. "You're still recovering. You do not have the energy needed to use your power. It could hurt you—burn you out. I can't ask you to—"

"You don't have to ask," I whisper.

Cal looks away, the muscle in his cheek ticking. "I promised to protect you. I forced this life on you. If anything happens to you…I just…I couldn't bear it."

"You didn't force me," I say with as much conviction as I can muster. "Our hearts brought me here. Our bond—which was decided by the gods—is what brought me here. I choose you. I choose us. And if that means fighting by your side to protect our people, then I choose that too."

"I need you to promise me something," he says, voice low. "If I fall—if this goes badly—you run. You will be safe with the wolves. Find the Nights and my sister. You will be safe there."

"No."

"Willa—"

"There is no me without you."

His eyes close like the words pain him more than anything else ever could.

"We share a heart now, Stud," I continue, pressing my palm to his chest. "The same rhythm, the same beat. Yours roars in me and mine sings in you. If you fall, I fall."

Cal's hand comes up to cover mine, warm and calloused and trembling. "You could survive. You could live."

"Without you? No thanks."

I take a deep breath and let my tears fall. "Your people are *my* people now, Cal. This world, this land, this forest, these mountains—they are mine too. I *know* I was brought here for a reason. My magic. I was given it for a reason. I will use it to protect what is *mine*."

He stares at me, fear and love and something wild sparkling in his eyes. "Even if it kills you?"

"If it saves them," I say, waving my hand in the direction of his friends and his home. "Then I'll die knowing I was finally exactly where I was meant to be. But I don't plan on going that easily. Do you?"

Cal wraps his arms around me, pulling me into his chest. I lean in, feeling our bond thrumming like a pulse between us.

"No running?" he whispers into my hair.

"No running," I whisper back. "We do this together."

Cal's lips press against the top of my head, and I feel the bear inside him rise, just as the storm of power inside me begins to swell.

We might meet death—but we will do it side by side.

And we will not go without a fight.

"Bo, retrieve their leader. If rescuing him from our dungeon is what has given them the balls to attack us head on, he should be out in the open," I order, before turning to Cal. "It might stop them from entering the keep."

Cal kisses my forehead before nodding to Bo to follow my command.

"Colt, where is Mira?" I ask.

"She is helping Cook hide those who cannot fight in the tunnels under the kitchen." he tells me.

I nod, thankful that my new friend will not be in the direct line of attack. "Then let's do this."

I walk hand in hand with Cal as we exit the safety of the keep and stalk closer to the meadow. Cal kisses me hard before shifting and lowering himself so that I can climb up his leg and settle onto his back.

Flanked by his cadre in their bear forms, I can't help but think how similar and yet utterly different this scene is from when I first arrived in this world. It may have seemed brave of me to throw myself into the fight by the lake, to put myself between the attacking bears and the bears who came to my rescue—but I thought it was all just a dream. I did not think that there would be any real consequences to my actions. But now I know. This is real. Absolutely unbelievable, but completely real. I do my best to steady my heart as we enter the field, knowing that we do not have much hope of coming out the victors in this battle.

"I love you," I say, knowing that Cal will hear me despite the wind stealing my words.

As we make our way to the center of the clearing, I allow my power to slowly pulse under my skin. It feels as though I have more control, despite my exhaustion. Every other time that I have used my magic, it has burst out of me as an act of desperation. But right now, it feels like a steady hum just under the surface.

Cal stops just as the enemy bears break through the tree line. Steeling myself, I force my shoulders back and keep my head held high. I refuse to cower. They do not deserve my fear.

The wind rips through the open field, carrying with it the scent of sweat, iron, and something older—something ancient. Cal once told me that the forest, the mountains, the land—it all carries power that has helped him throughout the years. As if The Mother is doing what she can to help.

Cal stands still beneath me, a mountain for fur and muscle under my thighs. His brown pelt bristles with tension, every breath through his massive chest reverberating up into my bones. But I welcome it all. I grip the thick scruff at the base of his neck, steadying myself in his presence. My bear. My family. My heart.

Across the field, a wall of enemy bears looms, each one a hulking mass of fury. There are too many. Dozens upon dozens. Behind them, the trees tremble like even the forest fears this day.

Then, one bear steps forward, claws shrinking, body contorting, until a man stands in its place. Tall, cruel, smug. Naked, other than the stolen gold that adorns his scarred skin and the arrogance of someone who truly believes the victory is already his.

His hand raises in the air, stopping the progression of his army. "Willa of the Otherworld," he calls, voice ringing with disdain and authority.

I snort. If we survive this day, I might have to keep that title.

"You have no claim here," he continues. "Surrender the keep, the prisoners, and the gold, and I may let you and your beast live."

I lean forward, glaring down from Cal's back. "You'll *let* us live?"

The man smiles thinly. "You are outnumbered ten to one. You were never meant to be here. And the beliefs of the Sun Kissed remaining in power are outdated. You are a novelty. Nothing more."

Slowly, I stand on Cal's back, balancing despite the wind whipping around me like a vortex of unrestrained power. Magic hums beneath my skin, the pulse of it building, swelling with my fury. "I may have come from another world, but these people—these bears—they are my family. And I will protect them."

His eyes narrow. "Then you will die with them."

I fling my hands forward, and with it comes a blast of light, a pulsing wave of magic that cracks the earth under their feet and sends the front line of enemy bears stumbling back. Not enough to kill. Not yet. But enough to remind them I am not powerless.

"Try me," I growl.

The man snarls, shifting back into his monstrous form with a sickening crunch of bone and sinew. Then comes the roar—dozens of them. The enemy surges forward.

And so do we.

Cal bolts beneath me, a growl ripping from his throat like thunder. We crash into their line with fang and fury. All around us is chaos. My pulses of magic explode outward, waves of raw force that knocks the enemies back—but even as I fight, even as I push, I cannot protect everyone.

All around me, our clan begins to fall, overwhelmed and overtaken. Each sending out a final roar before being dragged down and knocked out. I glance over to see Tor's body collapse on the field as five bears attack him head on. They quickly move on to their next victim, leaving his prone body lying on the blood-soaked earth. The subtle rise of his chest telling me that he is still alive.

Still, I fight. Still, I stand on Cal's back, emitting steady pulses of power as my energy depletes.

I don't know how much time passes before I notice that we are alone against our attackers. Just like that day by the lake, Cal and I are all that still stand. Except this time, my judgement is not clouded by the belief that I will simply wake up. If Cal and I fall, the entire clan will fall. I can't let that happen.

I feel Cal's body tremble beneath me—whether from blood loss or exhaustion, he does not have much time left. My arms sag to my side, weak from overusing my magic. Dropping down to sit, I cling to his back and press a kiss to the crown of his head, tasting blood, sweat, and fur.

"Together," I whisper, voice raw.

A roar rises in response—but it isn't Cal's.

"WILLA!"

The voice tears through the battlefield like lightning. My head snaps left, and my heart stutters.

Bounding over the hill is a sight I never dared to hope for.

Bears—hundreds of them—charging forward, kicking up dust. At their front, massive and terrifying, is a bear rivaling only Cal in size. Fur black as night, eyes glowing violet and gold with ancient magic. And on his back—fuck, I can't breathe.

"Freya!" I yell. Tears blur my vision at the sight.

Freya, alive and fierce, her hair braided and windswept, screams my name again.

At the sight of our reinforcements, the enemies halt, unsure what to do now that they are outnumbered.

I fall, sliding down Cal's legs and landing harshly. Freya meets me on the ground and our bodies collide, a fresh wave of tears soaking my cheeks. Wrapping my exhausted body up in her arms, we both collapse into a pile of tangled limbs and grateful sobs.

"You didn't think I'd let you fight alone, did you? Let's end this," she says, eyes shimmering with the same ancient power that hums in my veins. Hand in hand, we use our magic to force the enemy bears back. And together—finally *together*—we turn the tide.

33
Steeling Hearts

Callum

The air still stinks of blood, sweat, and battle. My ears ring with the echo of roars—ours and theirs—though the battlefield had long since gone silent. The sun now sits low, bleeding gold across the torn-up ground outside the keep walls, and I stand there, too worked up to fully shift back, my claws wet with the fight.

We should have died.
We would have.
If not for them.

I turn, staring at the empty field where hundreds of battle-ready warriors had stood just moments before. Casimir's army—fur bristling, eyes burning, the ground trembling under the weight of their charge. Now, all gone. All but ten. Like they'd been smoke in the wind, some divine flare snuffed out after the job was done.

"Cal," Willa's voice comes from behind me, soft but unafraid by my half-shifted form. Her hand brushes my arm and it is enough for my shift to pull back fully, bones cracking, skin knitting as I meet her gaze. Goddess, she is beautiful. Face smudged with blood and dirt, gold and moss eyes wide with everything she witnessed today, power humming under her skin like a bolt of lightning.

"Are you okay, my love?" I ask, even though the answer cannot be answered so simply. Nobody is alright. Not really.

Willa nods anyway. Liar. But I will let her lie, just this once.

Freya clings to her side, not wanting to separate for more than a moment. They hadn't seen each other since the accident—since that night Willa's world cracked wide open and she fell into my heart.

Caz stands beside them, quiet as ever, arms crossed over his chest, his eyes scanning the destruction. He catches my gaze and gives me a small nod, all warrior and leader, but his eyes are softer now. Like the edge had dulled just a little with Freya safe by his side. I wonder if my eyes show the same softness.

Later, when our injured are helped and our fallen have woken, we gather in the dining room. The stone walls still bear scars from the attack that took my family so many years ago, reminding me just how much we almost lost today.

The air in the room feels heavy. No longer with grief, but with purpose.

Willa sits on my lap, my hands holding her body tightly to mine. Reassuring me that she is okay. *We* are okay. Around the table, Tor, Bo, Adan, Colt, and Mira sit ready to tackle our next challenge. Our family. Our people. Most of us still bear wounds, wrapped in bandages or stiff with drying blood. None of us have the energy to pretend to be in better shape than we are.

Casimir leans forward, his voice low but clear. "You want answers. We will tell you what we can, but I must admit that there is a lot that we still do not understand. The prophecy that you wrote about, it is talking about our Mates. Freya, Willa, and I would bet my gold on Sol having a Mate in this world as well."

Tor makes a grunt of agreement before reciting the words of the prophecy for us all to hear:

> Symptoms of The Mother Cursed
> With Rapacity's Blight
> There will be Three Sons of the First
> Aided by a Sister's Might
> Who will Rise from the Shadows

Back into the Light
Together as One
Claw, Paw, and Maw
Will Fight the Bane
Will Start their Reign
And Rid The Mother of her Pain."

"Clans Claw, Paw, and Maw are all listed in the poem. That paired with 'Three Sons of the First, Aided by a Sister's Might,' tells me that we only make up two thirds of this puzzle," Caz adds.

"And your Sun Kissed magic allows you to conjure an army?" Willa asks Freya.

"Kind of," Freya explains. "From what I have been able to figure out so far, I am able to create illusions, like a magical trick of the light. I had never created such a large illusion before, but when I saw you about to fall, it kind of blasted out of me and multiplied in size."

"And then just went poof after," Willa adds.

Freya nods. "I can't maintain the illusion for long periods of time. I'm just thankful that I was able to hold onto it for long enough."

"I thought you died," Willa says quietly, no longer talking about the battle that we fought today. "The crash."

Freya exhaled shakily. "I did…in a way. We both did."

Silence fell, thick as fog as we all soak in her words.

"Our hearts restarted in this world after they went quiet back in Chicago. I...I didn't die on impact. Neither did Sloane. I don't know how you did it, but you shielded us. The doctors couldn't understand how it was possible. The car that hit us was going 70 miles per hour. I was pushed from the car. Now that I have seen your power, I think...well, I think maybe that was when you used your magic for the first time."

Willa gasps, clinging tighter to the arm that I have banded around her middle.

"And you woke up? How did you..."

"I was in a coma. I could hear the doctors and our families talking around me, but I wasn't awake. Not really. It was all too much strain on my heart. I saw a blinding light. I chose..." She shakes her head. "Something about the light made me feel like it would bring me home. And it did." Freya turns to look at Caz. He places a gentle kiss on her lips.

The room fell still again. All of us lost in thoughts of what was and what could have been. My eyes meet Caz's across the table, both of us understanding that we almost lost our Mates before we even had a chance to find them.

Colt finally breaks the silence. "What now?"

Freya looks at Willa. "Now, we learn. We train. We dig into the prophecy and find out what's coming next. Because today wasn't the end. It was just the beginning."

Willa turns in my arms, her eyes dark with determination.

I meet her gaze and nod once.

Let whatever is coming try.

We'd be ready.

And this time, we will not be alone.

Epilogue

Callum

The stairwell down to the dungeon is colder than it should be. It carries the kind of chill that sinks into bone, a damp, stone-heavy breath that presses against my skin even through the heat simmering under it.

My bear hates being here. Hates descending into a place where prey-scent hangs so thick we can taste it on our tongue.

But we cannot do a damn thing about it. Not yet.

Colt walks at my right, silent, but tension rides his shoulders like an iron yoke. Tor is at my left, jaw clenched so tight I hear his teeth grind. Their scents—loyal, furious, wounded—braid with mine in the narrow stairwell.

Family binds us all. But it betrays us just as easily.

Willa would remind me that *not all* family is to blame. And she is right. I know that. But after everything that my family, my clan, has already lost, this betrayal cuts deep.

I can hear her soft voice in my memory. The night she convinced me to delay my judgement, despite still wearing the physical marks of their treachery. The night she curled against my chest, heart still racing from her nightmares, and asked me to think—really think—before spilling more blood on Claw stone.

She believes mercy is a strength.

Some days, I think she might be right.

Today…I am not sure.

The torchlight flickers as we reach the bottom. The dungeon corridor opens like a throat—narrow, lined with black iron bars, echoing every footstep. The guards snap to attention, fists over hearts, heads bowed. Not in fear, but respect. The keep has not recovered from the rebel's attack or from the fact that two of our respected clan members plotted to murder my Heart Mate.

I give a curt nod as we pass them, stepping into the corridor.

The smell hits first—fear, stale sweat, desperation, and the faint sharp sting of regret.

Aurora sits in the first cell on the left, hair tangled but chin lifted as if she is the wronged one. Due to the size of the cells, my prisoners are unable to shift into their bear forms. It is intentional—denying them the comfort of their beast as well as the strength of their shifted form.

Arturas is in the cell next to her, spine rigid, shoulders proud despite his current condition.

Further down, the rebel leader—Cormac—rolls his neck like the bars are an inconvenience. And his daughter, Ciara, curls herself in the far cell, arms wrapped around her knees, eyes glazed over like she is no longer completely there.

Four lives.

Four choices.

And every one of them could break this clan all over again.

Colt steps in front of his father's cell. His breath comes out sharp. "Every time I see him in this cage, I wonder why we have not ended him yet," he mutters, not caring that his father is able to hear him.

Tor replies, a look of disgust crossing his face as he looks at his mother. "Because Cal listens to his Mate now. Which is better than they deserve."

I huff out a humorless breath. "Willa is not wrong to ask me to think before killing people."

Aurora scoffs immediately, loud enough to echo off of the stone walls. "You have gone soft," she sneers.

I turn my head slowly toward her, letting her see the shift in my eyes. "Soft?" My voice is low, steady. "If I were soft, aunt, you would not still be breathing."

Her bravado falters, just for a heartbeat.

Good.

I step closer, wrapping my hand around the iron bar between us. It creaks—a warning of my strength. "Willa asked for patience. She did not ask for mercy."

Aurora looks away.

Arturas clears his throat. "Chief—"

"Don't." Colt's voice lashes out, rough and raw. He does not even look at his father. "You do not get to speak to him like you still hold the right. You lost your position in this clan the moment you decided to trade an innocent life, the life of our Chief's Heart Mate, for a potential alliance that would have never come to fruition. The rebels would never have agreed to peace. Their avidity for power wouldn't allow it. And they would not have stopped with Willa. They would continue to take and take, demanding more and more, until every last drop of Sun Kissed blood was returned to The Mother."

Arturas stiffens, but he shuts his mouth.

Silence settles, broken only by the drip of water somewhere in the dark.

I let it stretch. Let them all feel it.

Because beneath my skin, my bear wants blood. It wants to end this—clean, final, permanent. But Willa's warmth remains coiled around my heart, whispering logic where instinct roars.

We do not know what killing Cormac triggers.

We do not know how fractured the rebel clans are now that he is captured.

We do not know if his daughter is a victim or an accomplice.

And I am not in the business of making more enemies out of ignorance.

When I finally speak, my voice is level. "I want to kill all four of you." Tor and Colt go still beside me, not surprised—just acknowledging. "If this choice were mine alone, this corridor would run red, becoming the tomb it was truly meant to be."

Aurora inhales sharply. Arturas looks away. Cormac only smiles.

Smug bastard.

"But," I continue, "Willa asked me to consider the cost of each life. And she is right. A dead enemy might create ten more. A dead traitor leaves questions behind. A dead girl—" I glance towards Ciara, "—might be the spark that lights another war."

Ciara flinches.

Cormac's jaw clenches.

Good. Let them feel each truth as it lands.

Tor steps forward, bracing his hands on the bars of his mother's cell. His voice is steady, but the pain beneath it is unmistakable. "You threatened the life of my Chief's

Heart Mate. My cousin's Mate. My clan's future. You would have let the rebels tear her apart like she was nothing. And now, that is what you are to me, mother. Nothing."

Aurora gasps, as if his words hurt more than the pain that she caused my Mate.

Arturas's voice comes out low. "We thought—"

"No," I snap. "You *wanted*. You did not think."

His mouth shuts with a click.

"Envy poisons slowly," I say, stepping between Colt and Tor, facing all four cells. "Greed does it faster. You two—" I nod toward Aurora and Arturus, "—spent years feeling inadequate. Letting your own shortcomings fester until you found a rhetoric to justify your actions. The rebels told you that our ways are outdated, and some of them might be, but not that of Heart Mates. And not that of Sun Kissed blessings. Your resentment grew like a disease. And you, Cormac." I turn to the rebel leader. "You use that resentment like kindling. You fan it into a wildfire. But you never stopped to notice how many innocent people you burned along the way."

His lip curls. "You speak of innocence like your clan never shed blood."

"My clan defends itself. Yours manipulates children into mindless weapons." My gaze slides to Ciara.

She wraps her arms tighter around her legs.

Cormac snarls. "Leave her out of this."

"You didn't." My answer is ice.

For a moment, the dungeon seems to hold its breath. Every prisoner watches me. Colt and Tor wait for my judgment.

Finally, I exhale.

My bear does not like the words forming, but they are the right ones.

"For now," I say, voice ringing through the corridor, "you will stay prisoners. All of you. No executions. No negotiations. No release."

Aurora's eyes widen. Arturas slumps. Corman bares his teeth in frustrated silence. Ciara lets out a breath that sounds like a sob.

Colt frowns. "You are sure?"

"No," I admit, turning on my heel to leave. "But certainty is not a luxury we have right now."

Tor nods slowly, falling into step at my side. "Willa will be relieved."

"She will be safe," I correct. "And that is what matters."

As we step into the echoing dark, I cannot help but let one final thought surface—a thought that tastes equal parts hope and bitterness.

Willa has not made me soft.

She has made me see clearly.

And what I see now is a future worth fighting for.

Author's Note

Writing this series felt like taking a deep, messy, magical breath right along with my characters. Watching them stumble, grieve, rage, and grow has been heartbreaking, hilarious, and surprisingly healing for me. They have reminded me that grief comes in all shapes and sizes and that friendship can carry you further than you expect.

It is probably hard to believe now, but Juniper's character almost didn't exist. I was about half-way through writing Nightfury when she pulled me out of a dream and insisted that I write her into the book. I'm sure that sounds crazy to most of you, but if you are a writer, you get it. Once her character took shape, I knew that *this* was the story that I needed to tell next.

For the readers returning from my first series, thank you from the bottom of my heart for your support. You've made it possible for me to keep exploring this world, keep falling in love with these characters, and keep writing the stories that make my heart—and hopefully yours—feel a little bigger.

And for those new to these pages, welcome! I can't wait to continue this adventure with you.

—Ruby Ellis

Also By
Ruby Ellis

The Moon Touched Chronicles
Nightfang (Rowan & War)
Nighthowl (Ramsey & Griffin)
Nightfury (Reese & Bade)

The Sun Kissed Scrolls
Light Claw (Willa & Callum)
Bright Paw (Freya & Casimir)

www.rubyellisauthor.com
www.tiktok.com/@author.ruby.ellis

Willa and Cal's book might be complete, but you don't need to say goodbye yet. Both characters will make frequent appearances in Casimir & Freya's story.

Keep reading for an exclusive sneak peek of Bright Paw, the second book in The Sun Kissed Scrolls trilogy.

1
The Invisible Life of Freya Banks

Freya

I used to think 'invisible' was just a metaphor. A dramatic word I used in the margins of my journals when I wanted to feel poetic. But now, floating somewhere between a heartbeat and nothingness, I realize invisibility is real. Not just a trick of the light. But a place. A condition. My eternal actuality.

The machines beside me hum and beep in rhythm, mechanical breaths that fill the silence between the doctor's words. He speaks softly, like people do when they think the dying might hear them. My mother sniffles. My father clears his throat.

"She's stable for now," the doctor says. "But the brain activity hasn't changed much since she arrived."

Well, that can't be good.

There's a pause thick enough to drown in. It isn't the first time that my lack of response has harshed the vibe.

"How much longer will we have to stay here?" My father asks. "I have a meeting tomorrow."

Of course he does. Even now, with tubes in my throat and a needle in my arm, he's thinking about quarterly reports and investors. I wish I could roll my eyes, maybe cough just to make him look at me. But my body is a locked door, and I don't have the key.

My mother's voice is tight, shaking in that way she gets before she starts to cry or drink—sometimes both. "What am I supposed to tell people?" she asks.

I can just picture the doctor's face—thinking that he was having a difficult conversation with my grieving, loving parents. But instead, he is forced to answer insensitive questions like *what is the socially acceptable amount of time to wait before pulling the plug?* And, *what will our friends at the club think about our daughter getting hit by a car because she was out until bar close?*

All of their words are thick with judgment.

I want to scream.

Not that the truth matters to them, but I wasn't drinking. Sloane and I were waiting for our friend, Willa's, shift to end so that we could give her a ride home. We were supposed to laugh about Sloane's dating misadventures and Willa's stories of what people confess when they have had one too many pints of Guinness. But instead, tires screeched, glass shattered, and now, I'm here.

And they're not.

The doctor said as much.

Willa was killed on impact, having tried to shield us from the speeding car. Sloane was stuck in the car as it went up in flames. She made it to the hospital but succumbed to her injuries shortly after.

Me? I was found outside of the car, like something had pushed me—removed me. It probably would have been a miracle if I could have landed on anything other than my head. So now I am just here. Listening. Fading.

Willa and Sloane were my only constants in a world that pretended I was decoration. We met in a church basement when we were children. Three little kids with heart defects. We used to joke that we were invincible because our hearts were already broken—how could we not survive everything else?

That was until the crash proved that even patched up hearts can stop beating.

My father sighs, impatient. "She shouldn't have been out that late anyway. She needs to take responsibility for her actions."

I want to laugh. A dry, brittle laugh that doesn't need air to breathe.

Responsibility? Hah! As if he has ever taken responsibility for anything in his life.

The doctor murmurs something about hope and recovery. About how it's too early to give up. He reminds them that I am only 25 years old. That I could wake up.

My mother scoffs at his suggestion that I could live a normal life. Not because he is suggesting that I could come out of this okay but because she doesn't believe I could ever live up to their version of normal, even before the accident.

A mid-sized, independent woman who would rather hide away in my art studio than get my ass grabbed by whatever business partner my father has around? Scandal.

Normal has never been the standard that they set for me. Neither was *happy*.

I start to drift, still floating in the nothingness but falling further into the deep.

It's strange how being unseen feels familiar—comforting. It shouldn't, but my whole life has been a quiet rehearsal for this moment. Sitting at dinner while my parents performed their version of perfection. Ignoring the long line of mistresses and pills that they used to dull their own inadequacies. Smiling through it all, as if it could just be forgotten if it is ignored. Like me.

Even now, I'm the centerpiece of the room, the reason they're here, and yet I'm still invisible.

I want to move.

I want to open my eyes.

I want to trade their apathy for a few minutes of quiet.

But then something changes.

The machines fade into a soft hum. The voices into whispers. And there it is—a light. Bright to the point of blindness, but vital to everything that I am. It feels warm. Gentle. Forgiving.

There is no fear. No hesitation. Just a pull—like gravity in reverse.

For once, I don't think about what my parents will say or how the papers will phrase the accident. I don't think about being invisible or broken or unloved.

I think about Willa's laugh. I think about Sloane's stupid puns.

I think about how alive we felt just hours ago.

And then I walk forward.

Into the light.

Into something that finally—*finally*—sees me.

www.ingramcontent.com/pod-product-compliance
Lightning Source LLC
LaVergne TN
LVHW010311070526
838199LV00065B/5521